Charles Wolcott Balestier

The Average Woman

Captain, my Captain!

Charles Wolcott Balestier

The Average Woman
Captain, my Captain!

ISBN/EAN: 9783743312982

Manufactured in Europe, USA, Canada, Australia, Japa

Cover: Foto ©Andreas Hilbeck / pixelio.de

Manufactured and distributed by brebook publishing software (www.brebook.com)

Charles Wolcott Balestier

The Average Woman

CONTENTS

WOLCOTT BALESTIER

THEY have a place apart in the record of the
dead, the young names which represent less
for the big indifferent public than for a knot
of friends who remember and regret, and yet
on behalf of which we discreetly plead for
some attenuation, in the general memory, of
the common fate. So far as they *are* spared
by oblivion they form a ghostly but enviable
little band––the company of those who were
estimated early and rescued early, who created
expectations and cherished hopes, and for
whom there remains no question of disappointment or of failure. We can think of
them as it most pleases us to think, allude to
them with unchallengeable faith, and give

our imagination the luxury of filling out the vague disc of the possible. Charles Wolcott Balestier, who died in Dresden on the 6th of December 1891, just before he had reached his thirtieth year, participates in this dim distinction, and becomes one of the mute appealers to whom we are indulgent in proportion as we recognise that what there is to "show" for them accounts but imperfectly for our plea. We make the plea for the plea's sake, and because that is fairer than not to make it. He had not had time, though he had so many of the other conditions, and this particular use of a little of the time that we ourselves feel half-ashamed to have gained—as if we had gained it at his expense—presents itself as an act of common generosity.

Wolcott Balestier loved literature better than anything but his friends, and he had found opportunity to testify to this in a career as eagerly active as it was short. He left behind him a youthful unpublished novel, which is, conspicuously, to see the light; three very short tales, and the vivid mark of his collaboration with Mr. Rudyard Kipling in *The Naulahka*. His memory therefore may take its stand on a certain quantity of performance; but I confess that it is not mainly under the impression of this little sum of literary achievement that I find myself moved to speak of him. What he wrote, what he would have published, will be largely and sympathetically scrutinised, but there are persons for whom it will remain both only the smaller part of what he did and the pledge of a talent smothered at the very moment it had begun to expand. He was conscious that he had only begun, and it would be an unkindness to his memory to represent that, in spite of the extreme vividness of "Reffey" and of "Captain, my Captain!" his slender relics were very sacred in his own eyes. They are interesting, and

in glimpses original, but their greatest merit
is perhaps that by making him for the hour an
actuality they give us a pretext for attempting
to preserve some little record of his benefi-
cence. He was a man of business of
altogether peculiar genius, and it was in this
light that he figured, with singular intensity,
to a large number of charmed, befriended
people during the part of his brief life in
which I judge that he had lived more than in
all its preceding time, the three crowded
London years that began in December 1888.
This was the period of my acquaintance with
him ; my personal relations with him became
close, and I speak of him, of course, essentially as I had the good fortune to know him.
I freely confess that I should not add my
voice to the commemorative hum if it were a
question of taking any less affectionate a
point of view.

I speak of his having " figured " in London,
because he was from the first, in his bright

x

young ingenuity, his suggestion of immediate capacity, an apparition essentially salient. This was what he remained to the end, unmistakably an influence exotic and curious, dropped down from without, not thrown up from within. He made London, on the ground on which he dealt with it, so extraordinarily his own that the contrast between the spirit and the matter, the agent and the medium, could only grow more striking and, if I may frankly say so, more amusing. Nothing feeds more actively some of our reflections than the sight of that animated symbol, the "cultured American," entangled for the first time in the dense meshes of the great London net. The manner in which his native faculty deals with them is often an instructive spectacle. We see it, however, for the most part, exercised in a merely contemplative or "sight-seeing" way, in the interest of leisure and shopping, or at the most of patriotism and consolation. But Wolcott

Balestier, at twenty-seven, with a very complicated and characteristic American past already behind him—born at Rochester, N.Y., in 1861, he had haunted colleges, administered libraries, started "businesses," explored territories, conducted theatricals, edited periodicals and published "works"— this penetrating representative of a peculiarly transatlantic interest in books alighted in the formidable city, in the dusky void of Christmas week, on no merely passive errand. He had a specific mission, business to transact for an American publishing firm, but I trust I do no injustice to the perfection with which he transacted it if I say that such things could, in the nature of the case, give him only his pretext and his introduction. What he had really come for, as it turned out, was to find a field large enough for his admirable spirit. The field was largest in London because London was an extension without being a substitution. It "took in," as it were, the

great agglomerations he had left beyond the
sea, and added others to them. It had in a
word—it always has—the advantage of being
the biggest box at the theatre, the highest seat
of observation of the English-speaking multi-
tude as a whole— with nothing less than which
was Wolcott Balestier prompted to concern
himself.

I met him, accidentally, soon after his
arrival, and was struck with his happy perceptions and with his acute appreciation of
London. Young and fresh as he was, he
rejoiced in the dim vastness of the great city
—this was a quality which he found altogether
inspiring. He delighted in space and number, and dealt with the latter element in
particular in a way which, at his age, was
already masterly. He never was so happy as
when he had too many things to do, and he
could view the infinite multiplication of detail with pure exhilaration. This is partly
what I mean by his admirable spirit, which

was his love of handling large things, of handling everything in a large way. In the poor little three years to which the best of his activity was restricted he of course had estabished but imperfectly his independence; but they were sufficient to give the measure of his capacity. It was those who knew him best who "chaffed" him most about his Napoleonic propensities—his complete incapacity to recognise difficulties, his immediate adoption of his own, or, in other words, of an original solution. It never could have occurred to him that there was not a way round an obstacle so long as a way was inventible, and the invented way, which in almost all cases was the one he embraced—he suspected stupidity, with which he had no patience, in the readymade—always proved in fact the most amusing. This was a high recommendation to him, for, observant and genial as he was, he liked to enjoy transactions for themselves, as one is happy in the exercise of an implanted faculty, quite apart from purpose and profit. The Copyright Bill had not yet been passed, and it appeared to him that there might be much to be done in helping the English author in America to a temporary *modus vivendi*. This was an idea at the service of which he put all his ingenuity—an ingenuity sharpened by his detestation of the ignoble state of the law. This acute and sympathetic interest in the fruits of literary labour, as they concern the labourer, generalised and systematised itself with extraordinary rapidity, and became, by the time he had been six months in London, a very remarkable and singularly interesting passion, a passion which, for those who had the advantage of seeing it in exercise, quickly assumed all the authority of genius.

It was a faculty altogether individual, and one of the most original I have ever known. It consisted, in its simplest expression, of an extraordinary agility in putting himself in the place of the man, and quite as easily, when the need was, of the woman, of letters ; and it sprang from an intense and curious appreciation of the literary character and an odd, charmed, amused acceptance of the dominion of the book.   Nothing could be quite ultimate for a spirit so humorous, but Wolcott Balestier found in the importunity of the book the elements of a kind of cheerful fatalism, a state of mind that went hand in hand, in a whimsical way, with the critical instinct.   To see the book through—almost even through the press—was a perpetual pastime to him, and one that varied of course according to what the book might be.   It was far greater in some cases than in others ; but in the free play of his ingenuity he could *faire un sort*, prepare a kind of respectable future, for almost anything newly printed and published, take a peep from any point of view that passed muster as literary.   In this way, in our scribbling hours, he multiplied immensely his relations with the pendriving class, even in the persons of some of its most pathetic representatives, of whom he became, in the shortest space of time, the clever providence and kindly adviser. Signs were not wanting from many of these after his death, signs of their mourning for him as the most trusted of friends. And all this, on the young man's part, in a spirit so disinterested and so sincerely sympathetic that one hardly knew what name to give to the genius of the market when the genius of the market appeared in a form so human.

He had the greatest appetite for success, and had begun to be a man of business of the very largest conceptions, but I have never seen this characteristic combined with so visible an indifference to the usual lures and ideals of commerce. As the faithful representative of others, he could only be jealous of their interests, but a high and imaginative talent for affairs could not well have been associated with less reverence for mere acquisition. He had in fact none at all—he seemed to me to care nothing for money. What he cared for was the drama of business, the various human game. To make money, up to a certain point, would have been convenient to him, and if he proposed to do so it was simply because this meant freedom—freedom to make a very different use of his time when (at no very distant day, as he hoped), the hour should strike. Much as he was absorbed in the literary affairs of other people, he was excusable for keeping a commodious chamber of his brain open to his own; and he had the most definite purpose of hammering away at the modern, the very modern novel, as soon as he should get out of the glare of the market-place and be able to command the conditions. He had already given pledges in this direction—had published two boyish fictions before coming to England, and in the intervals of his busy first year in London had put together a long story of much maturer, of really confident promise. An intimate personal alliance with Mr. Rudyard Kipling had led to his working in concert with that extraordinary genius, a lesson precious doubtless and wasted, like so many of his irrepressible young experiments—wasted, I mean, in the sense of its being a morning without a morrow.

Wolcott Balestier's death came too soon, in my judgment, to permit of a just calculation of what he might have done; we must recognise the limits of the evidence that his talent was real and remarkably capable of growth—evidence confirmed, on the part of those who knew him, by the sense of his acuteness and his ambition. He was all for the novel of observation, the undiscourageable study of the actual; he professed an intense relish for the works of Mr. Howells and there is little reason to doubt that if he had lived to give what was in him the followers of some

of the ancient ways would have had many a
bone to pick with him. The prospect of
picking such bones was, for himself, a thing
to add zest to the existence he was not
destined to enjoy. His imagination, so far as
he had given a hint of it, was all American,
and a long stay in the Far West, a familiarity
with mining-camps and infant cities, had
given it, for the time at least, the turn of the
new convention. He was prejudiced in favour
of American humour—it was his only pre-
judice that I can remember; fortunately it is
not one that is fatal to intellectual growth.
He liked little raw new places only one degree
less than he liked London, where he had
established himself, in the heart of West-
minster, under the Abbey towers, just within
the old archway of that Dean's Yard which
makes a kind of provincial backwater, like the
corner of a cathedral close, in a roaring
"imperial" neighbourhood. But when once
it had begun to go, his talent would pro-

xx

bably have had many moods and seasons. I remember thinking (on first observing what dreams he had of becoming a literary artist), that as the presumption is always against the duplication of a special gift, it was not particularly probable that the subtle secret of creation had been vouchsafed to a man who, in his natural mastery of affairs, might already account himself fortunately equipped. What community was there, in the same mind, between the noisy world of affairs and the hushed little chamber of literary art? That question was eventually answered—there could be none unless such a mind should be a rare exception. This was indeed the fact with Wolcott Balestier, and it made him, in my experience, unique.

I have known literary folk who were full, for themselves, of the commercial spirit, but I have in no other case known a commercial connection with literature to have had a twinship with an artistic one. Wolcott Balestier,

however, was commercial, as I may say, for
others; it was for himself that he cherished
the hope of achieving some painted picture of
life. Moreover, the technical term seems
invidious as applied to a part played so easily
and gracefully, with such friendly personal
perceptions. This function cost him nothing
intellectually—it was too instinctive and, in-
cidentally, as I have said, too suggestive. It
had advantages from the point of view of
what he intended when a better day should
have begun; it meant perpetual contact
with the world of men and women and
innumerable opportunities for observation.
In this he ironically exulted, and indeed it
made him enviable. He had a particular
aptitude for the personal part of affairs, for
arranging things in talk and face to face. He
had instincts and ideals of rapidity, and a
talent for dispensing with the matter of course
(which seemed to him flat and prosaic), cal-
culated often to bewilder the children of a

postponing habit. And it was given to him, moreover, to encounter the human, not to say the supposedly literary spirit, bared of factitious graces, in the simple severity of some of its appetites. He saw many realities and had already learned not to blink many uglinesses. Young as he was, he had perceived what was of the essence. He was a well of discretion, and it was charming and interesting in him, that even when he was most humorously communicative his talk was traversed by little wandering airs of the unsaid; nevertheless, he was not without nameless anecdotes and illustrations of this same tenacity of grasp— all the more striking that in general no man could be less prejudiced in favour of the publishing interest. Such an incident as the quick foundation of the " English Library " —an association for the larger diffusion on the Continent of English and American books —not only was a remarkable example of his fertility of resource (his idea always became a fact as soon as he could personally represent it and act for it), but brought with it an extension of experience of the sort which was really most remunerative to him, and as to which he could be independently and delightfully descriptive. It was partly on business connected with this happy undertaking and partly exactly to do nothing at all—to rest from a torment of detail and a strain of responsibility—that he made, sadly unwell when he started, in November 1891, that excursion to Germany from which he was not to return. He had only once or twice in his life been gravely ill, but those who were fond of him were never persuaded by his gallantry of optimism about himself, reinforced as it was by a thoroughly consistent and characteristic ingenuity in neglecting dull precautions, to think of his slender structure as really adequate to the service—the formidable service—of his generously restless spirit. It was not, in fact, and the disparity made him touching — makes his present image so in memory, though he doubtless would have carried on the brave deception much longer had it not been for the miserable typhoidal infection, from an undiscoverable source, that he bore with him from London, and to which, in happy unconsciousness, he succumbed.

It is vain to attempt to exclude the egotistical note from a memorial like the present, and the better course is frankly to enjoy the benefit of it. I may therefore mention that during the last year of his life in particular I saw him so often and so closely that, as I write, my page is overscored with importunate reminiscence and picture. These things are the possession of the private eye, but one would fain reflect something of their clearness in one's words. A wet winter night in a windy Lancashire town, for instance—a formidable "first night" at a troubled provincial theatre to which he had made a long and loyal pilgrimage for purposes of "support" at a

grotesquely nervous hour—such an occasion
comes back to me, vividly, with the very
quality of the support afforded, lavish and
eager and shrewd ; with the pleasantness of
the little commemorative inn-supper, half-
histrionic and wholly confident, and with the
dragged-out drollery of the sequel next day,
our sociable, amused participation in a collec-
tive theatrical fitting, effected in pottering
Sunday trains, besprinkled with refreshment-
room impressions and terminating, that night,
at an all but inaccessible Birmingham, in
independent repose and relaxed criticism.
He had taken, the summer before his death,
a house on the Isle of Wight—on the
south shore, well on the way to the Freshwater end—and I cannot withhold the
emphasis of and allusion to a couple of
August days spent there with him. One of
them had a rare perfection, and made the
purest medium for the high finish—as if it
were a leaf out of an old-fashioned drawing-

book—of the little pencilled island. It was given all to a long drive to Freshwater, much of the way over the firm grass of the great downs, and a lunch there and a rambling lazy lounge on the high cliffs, with the full sense of summer, for once, in a summerless year, and a still lazier return in the golden afternoon, amid all sorts of delicacies of effect of sea and land. He loved the little temporary home he had made on the edge of the sea, and even the great wind-storms of the early autumn, and no season of his life, probably, in spite of haunting illness, had given him more contented hours. Now he lies in the last place he could have dreamed of, the bristling alien cemetery, contracted and charmless, of the foreign city to which he had made his feverish way only to die. There was something in him so actively modern, so open to new reciprocities and assimilations, that it is not fanciful to say that he would have worked originally, in his degree, for civilisa-

tion. He had the real cosmopolitan spirit,
the easy imagination of differences and hin-
drances surmounted. He struck me as a bright
young forerunner of some higher common con-
veniences, some greater international trans-
fusions. He had just had time to begin, and
that is exactly what makes the exceeding pity
of his early end.

HENRY JAMES.

REFFEY

I

DAVE LEWIS ran passenger train No. 14 over the range one day, and brought back passenger No. 3 the next. No. 14 dined at Topaz and suppered at Mitcham's, as they said on the road ; No. 3 reversed the arrangement. He was required to report his train from Mitcham's, where he knew the manager of the eating-house, and the telegraph-operator. Both were young women.

For the last two months Reffey Deacon had not been sending in meals to the telegraph-operator when she was busy. For the same length of time Mattie Baker had forgotten to

send Reffey's provision order to Denver until
the next day. Reffey used the post now, and
Mattie came to the hotel dining-room for her
meals, like anybody else. Lewis had jilted one
girl for the sake of the other.

The two lived alone at Mitcham's ; other than
the servants, they were the only inmates of the
house and the entire population of the town,
which began and ended at the eating-station.
Their nearest neighbours lived ten miles away,
on a ranch up among the hills behind the hotel.
The front windows of the hotel looked out on a
cliff. It was a thousand feet high, and Reffey
and Mattie did not see the sun in the mornings
until it shone vertically down into their nest.
The eating-station, which was also a hotel, had
been placed at the exit from Red Rock Cañon,
as being the only spot within thirty miles large
enough to accommodate it. The floor of the
valley—lying between the cañon wall on one
side and the hills that climbed, beyond the
river, toward a rugged grazing country on the

2

other—was not above a couple of hundred yards in width ; the structure which the railway company had erected on this grudging space was an oblong frame building two stories high, painted a railroad grey, and containing only ten practicable bedrooms, in addition to the big dining-room, the refreshment-room, and the ticket-office and telegraph-office, occupying the ground-floor. But in the cañon, through which the railway had stolen a perilous way, there was room for nothing larger than the huts of flag-men or track-walkers ; and these structures were likely to hang out over the river, propped at the fringe of the ledge along which the track wriggled and balanced. In the summer parties of fishermen came to whip the Red Rock River, the stream that boiled and shouted through the cañon, and rooted night and day at the base of the rock on which the hotel was built. Holiday parties from the East, railroad-men in special cars, and English tourists, armed with expensive guns, also came at certain times, and spent a

3

week or two at Mitcham's troubling the echoes
among the hills. But at other seasons the two
women lived alone. The situation demanded
an amiable relation between them, and it was
intolerable without it.

Dave and Reffey were to be married as soon
as he could build her a proper house at
Maverick. Reffey (the name represented her
mother's fantastic shortening of Rebecca) had
her own ideas regarding a fit residence, and was
in process of imposing them upon Dave and
upon his builder. Lewis was now " knocking
down " more fares than before his engagement
to Reffey; instalments on the house were
coming due; he was beginning to look at
furniture; and Reffey was in other ways an
expensive young lady. Her standard of the
presents to be expected from a lover in Dave's
position was high.

The drummers, who had dared each other
for a month to try it on with Lewis when he
had first been promoted from the ticket-office

4

at Denver, smiled at each other now when they met, and they winked at Lewis. Lewis, on these occasions, fixed his eye intently on the ticket in the hands of the passenger in the next seat, keeping the responsive wink for the baggage-car, the upper corner of the smoker and the refreshment-counter at way-stations, where he came by cigars and drinks easily. Drummers who had once, long ago, stayed over a train or spent an extra night in a town rather than travel by his train, now exchanged jokes with him on the purity of his first month's work on the road. The atmosphere was easy-going and friendly on Dave Lewis's train now that they all knew him for one of the boys, and the men who had lost money by betting during that first month that he had been put on the road by the company to spot the crooked work of other conductors, now made him stand treat.

Dave asked them what they had taken him for, and they asked him how he expected them to tumble all at once to the fact that he was one of themselves when he came straight from the Denver ticket-office. They quoted the other conductors as having shared their idea, and they wanted to know why he had kept them so long in suspense.

"Why, boys, to tell the truth, I was the young and blushing maiden of that situation. I had to wait until I was asked."

"The drooping violet of Maverick—that's what you were—the shy little Denver Daisy. Remember the cigars and talky-talk I wasted on you before I got up sand to offer you three dollars for a five-dollar fare? One seventy-five is all you get out of me these days, you old fraud. We've got to make you sweat somewhere for that shrinking violet business—eh, boys? Well, here's my regards!"

Einstein, whose line was cloaks and trimmings, blew the foam off his beer and drank to Dave.

These regular patrons of the road (who were

6

accustomed to take the trains run by the right sort of fellow, without purchasing a ticket, paying a proportion of the fare to the complaisant conductor, who in his turn pocketed the entire sum, and made nothing of such amusing passengers in his report to the company), these steady customers of the company, forgave themselves slowly for their obtuseness ; but since the suspicion had been lifted from Lewis, they made it a point of honour to treat him as if it had never been. Now that they had proved his innocence, there was not a more popular conductor on the road. It was true that he was not thought exclusive enough since his engagement to Reffey. He now distributed his favours over a wider area, and almost any traveller who was a little "fly" could make a deal with him. It was a poor system for the company, but it worked well for Reffey; and if Dave ever had any doubts about it from a moral point of view, they were more than solaced in her society. The company charged passengers too much

7

and paid him too little, so that whichever way
he looked at it he was a remedial agent ; this
was probably the dumb reasoning with which
he satisfied his conscience. But, on the whole,
it would be easier to say how a murderer
excuses his crime than how a man sophisticates
such stealings. The one point clear to Dave
was that they were *not* stealings. Certainly
he never called them so, and since no one else
did, since even the company had no word for
practices of this nature, and no remedy for
them but dismissal, and since cases like his
never got into the courts, nor even, oddly
enough, into the newspapers, he was at liberty
to create his own moral world. In this world
he and his wants were easily chief, and the
railway (from which everything you got was so
much clear gain, and even clear righteousness,
yet which was, conveniently too, a disem-
bodied, soulless, dividend-paying corporation,
that nothing could injure) was easily last.

Reffey had not been able to help letting Dave

8

see from the first that she cared for him. It had begun on the day she arrived from Topeka (where she had acted as head-waitress of a hotel) to take charge of the eating-house at Mitcham's; and it may have been her evident preference for him which first flattered him into treason to Mattie. But his passion for her had not long needed a better reason than her own charms; once within the immediate range of them her beauty inflamed him, and he was snared by the strange, gipsyish, baleful witchery of a temperament scarcely more different from Mattie's than from his own. Her imperious, ardent loveliness ruled and fascinated him; Mattie's housekeeperly order of spirit and blessed calm of mind had merely cradled him.

He found the excitement of being engaged to Reffey a strain at times on a slow, mild disposition, the actual need of which was a peaceful harbour, but, save when his conscience accused him for his faithlessness to Mattie's simple trust,

he was aboundingly happy in the change. The
characteristic quality of his feeling for Reffey
was a huge admiration, and if he had been a
woman, and she a man, he would have crawled
at her feet ; as it was he let her worship him.
But he continued to admire her. After a
month's engagement she remained wonderful
and inscrutable to him ; entirely apart from his
love, he couldn't help feeling that he had made
an astonishing bargain. Whatever else might
happen she was sure to remain the only person
off her own piece of goods ; and it was from
this point of view, rather than out of the usual
lover's feeling of his unworthiness, that he tried
to live up to her. Every act of his life was
penetrated with the thought of her, and none
more than his daily reckoning up of his accounts
with the company.

He was accustomed at the end of the day to
find his way to the last seat in the smoker,
which was likely to be vacant, and to pour out
upon it the contents of his pockets, consisting

of the tickets and money gathered from passengers on the trip. After counting and noting
the tickets for his report, he told over the money
for what he called a "division of the spoils."
In these divisions, to which but one of the bene-
ficiaries was a party, the company "got what
was right"—that is, a little more than the least
it was likely to accept without grumbling. But
delicate questions often arose: there was not
always enough to go around ; the point of safety
was not definite, nor was it invariable ; it wasn't
even ascertainable, for yesterday's return might
have aroused suspicion, while, on the contrary,
it might have been so large as to form the germs
of habit in the company mind. The business
had its good and its bad days, like another ;
when " commercial " travel was large, and Dave
encountered other friends besides his drummers,
the day was a success : if to this was added, by
chance, a considerable flock of passengers who
had forgotten to buy their tickets, and who paid
the full fare in the simplicity of their hearts (he

gave them a duplex ticket, of course, but all contributions helped the exchequer), Dave re-marked mellowly to himself that it was " a good day for ducks." If it had been possible to keep trade up to a really high standard, Dave would have become shortly a Railway King, by methods not widely dissimilar from those generally recognised ; but, with all its faults, it remained a lucrative business.

He liked best to divide with the company when he was making the Western run, as every moment, in this case, brought him nearer to the object of these divisions, and to the object of all that he did. On these days he would usually begin his reckoning at the eastern end of the cañon, that he might know when he saw her what he had been able to do for her that day, even though he couldn't speak of it to her.

He celebrated an unusually good day by treating himself to the best cigar that had been given him on the trip, lolling back on the front seat of the smoker, and making pictures of the smoke during the long run through the cañon, in which no stations occurred to disturb him. After a thirty-dollar day he usually put another story on the house, in these reveries, bought the big Persian rug which he had envied at Daniel's and Fisher's in Denver, laid it on the parlour floor, seated Reffey in a deep wicker-chair on top of it, made the dull, rich red of the rug harmonise with the bronze red of her complexion, and with the flush of happiness on her cheek, caused her eye to rove from the rug to the furniture (red plush to match the rug—lots of gold on the chair legs), and from the furniture to the bright blaze he lighted on the hearth (their hearth !), and from the hearth to himself. The look of gratitude and love she gave him made his head swim in his vision, and not to stint himself, he closed the scene by making her give him a royal hug of her own accord, just as the whistle sounded for Mitcham's—and, down at the end of the cañon, Reffey was taking her place behind the lunch-counter.

On the days when Dave brought No. 14 over
the range from the East, Reffey went about her
usual occupations with an attent ear. Long
before the train came in sight on the bridge by
which it crossed the river a couple of hundred
yards from the hotel, a whistle rolled down to
her out of the heart of the cañon, multiplied in
howling echoes. The whistle went to her heart,
and, wherever she was, her dining-room girls
would see her pause in her quick, commanding
movements, arrested like a listening deer.
Then she would go on proudly, giving the last
neat touches to the dining-room tables, over
which a hungry riot was immediately to sweep.
A girl who had giggled in her palm one day
when the whistle blew had shrunk away,
scorched by a dozen words from Reffey, and
had left Mitcham's that night, with her trunk,
on the up-mixed-freight.

No. 14 stopped twenty minutes at Mitcham's,
and the better part of the passengers for this
reason preferred a regular supper in the hotel

14

dining-room to the chances of the lunch-counter. It was therefore from behind this comparatively unfrequented counter that Reffey usually directed her smile of greeting at Dave; the counter was of marble, and the triangular slices of pie were on the plates, the beans waited under their covers, and the ham sandwiches reared their pile of masonry.

She had spent a nervous half-hour behind this counter one warm spring afternoon, waiting for the whistle (she couldn't, of course, ask Mattie how late the train was), when the resounding blast always given, under arrangement, by Dave's engineer, leaped on her ear. As the echoes began to roll back on themselves into the cañon she gave a last polishing rub to the glass bell protecting her jelly-cake, trimmed the spirit-lamp under her monster coffee-urn, and put up a hand to the bunch of green bananas over her head to stop it twirling. Then she leaned over the counter, on her elbows, between the sandwiches and the cake to nod happily to Dave, as his train rolled up to the solitary eating-house and he followed his passengers in.

In this attitude he restrained himself with difficulty from giving her a real hug—she looked so splendidly, satisfyingly beautiful to him. As a matter of fact, Reffey was unmistakably handsome in her large arc-lamp fashion. She had uncommonly brilliant and beautiful eyes, passionate, liquid, beguiling, and shiningly resolute. Her face was not delicate, but it was strong with the same glow one saw in her eyes —a glow slightly crude, and perhaps more than slightly vicious, but richly alive. As she leaned over the counter her black, fluffy hair seemed nearer her heavy eyebrows than usual, her forehead looked lower, and her broad shoulders and abundant figure lost none of their value. She had a square, man's chin and decided compressed lips. She was carefully dressed, as was usual with her, in a figured cambric, without the apron worn by her dining-room girls.

16

She threw a smile at him, and began at the same time to attend rapidly and capably to the orders humbly suggested to her by the dozen passengers who had chosen the lunch-counter in preference to the dining-room. Dave threw a leg over the last stool in the row before the counter, and waited, with his elbows on the marble, for her to hand him the tender loin-steak and fried potatoes she was accustomed to keep for him. The steak came up through the dumb-waiter in a moment, smoking hot, and their hands met under the plate, as she set it down before him.

"What's Henry McKelway come up on the seven for?"

"To take my train to Portoe's Junction," returned Dave, with a smile. "It's a change-off I fixed up with him. Any objection?"

She looked up from the plate and pretended to examine the idea disinterestedly.

"Just as livs," she said, as she swept a bewildering smile over her adorer, who shivered where he sat with a sensation of pure joy.

She turned from him to snatch a bottle of St. Louis lager from a shelf high above her head. Dave wanted to vault over the counter, pull it down for her, and take her about the waist in just this attitude. Instead, he watched her, as she stood on tiptoe, swing her arm up to it with the sureness and grace of all her movements, and deposit it before him, after whirling it once in the air under the counter and catching it by the neck, with a laughing glance at him. Then, without another look in his direction, she moved away to attend to other customers, only returning to ask as he finished his steak and his lager :

"Want some pie—mince, apple, blackberry, blueberry, pumpkin, custard ?" She radiated love at him through her waitress manner : and Dave, giving back her look, dreamed into forgetfulness of pie, until she called herself back with a sharp "Well?"

"Ain't you got none of my patent brand?"

"Not allowed. Bad for the complexion."

"It ain't hurt yours any as I notice."

"Just you mind your own complexion, Dave Lewis."

"I use Madame Neckar's Frozen Balm night and morning. What do you want? Say, gimme some of that lemon meringue pie, now, you, and be quick about it."

She remained staring imperturbably at him through her lustrous, laughing eyes.

Dave knotted his fingers under the hand she spread out on the counter. "Come," he said worshippingly, "get a move on, will you?"

She popped her head under the counter and drew forth the double slice of thick lemon pie she had been keeping for him

"There, Greedy!" she said affectionately, under her breath, as she slid it toward him over the marble, with the twist she used for customers.

When the train had gone on in charge of

McKelway, and Reffey had straightened up her lunch-counter, she put on a sun-hat and followed him along the track toward the bridge over the river. The hat was large and daringly trimmed, but it became her exceedingly, and during the first minutes of their walk she used all the advantage it gave her over his stunned admiration.

She stepped from tie to tie with a long, free, swinging step, taking two ties at a time, while Dave contented himself with one. Mattie, watching them from the window of her telegraph-office, told herself sadly that they were a fine couple, and Reffey, glancing at Dave as they walked, said to herself that he *was* handsome. Dave was straight and well made; his face had the regular beauty, his black hair the fetching curl, his fine eyes the appealing, tender, conquering light which women love. He had, moreover, the gallant carriage of a calling in which, more than in almost any vocation of peace, except that of a sea-captain, a man gains

20

the habit of command and of responsibility. His train was always going on or stopping at his word, in Reffey's thought of him ; when he was away from her she pictured him with an authoritative hand in the air, waving his train forward or back, or, with a despotic lantern, flashing upon the engineer orders that might kill or save a hundred souls. She found no difficulty in reconciling his careful habit of dress to this conception of an heroic calling ; that touched the social side of his work, which demanded that a man shouldn't look like a fright in taking up tickets from ladies and gentlemen. She liked his little air of correctness, and the black clothes, which made him singular among men engaged in ordinary affairs and even a little singular among his fellow-conductors, the heavy gold watch-chain, the accurate, flat, black bow which he wore under his celluloid collar at an angle not intended to conceal the rhinestone collar-button above it ; above all she liked his crisp, jaunty, almost rakish moustache.

Reffey, who often took the airs of a good-
natured Czarina with him, now made him
account to her for every minute that had passed
since they had last met ; and in return, with the
charming condescension of the President's wife
talking to a master mechanic, gave him the
news of the road, of which she often knew more
than he by reason of her favourable post of
observation. Every brakeman, conductor,
engineer, and fireman on the Topaz division
passed her eating-house regularly, and as all
trains stopped, and as the trainmen were in-
timately dependent on her good-nature for the
quality of their meals, her shrewd eye and ear
had their opportunities. She made the men talk,
listening, watching and deducing pitilessly. Her
judgments were harsh ; she did not believe in
people. It was, perhaps, for this reason that she
believed with such abandonment in Dave—with
a kind of prostration and abasement with a total
and unreckoning gift of a nature wildly proud.

To both of them the road was a world ; they

thought of its hundreds of miles as having a local existence, and all their speech recognised the people who officered and worked it as the population of a single community. Both knew every person employed by the railway, his history, his present situation, and his prospects, as if he had been their fellow-townsman. They did not always sleep in the same place, this town population, but they all slept sometimes in the same place, and, going or coming, they all took the same meal at the same time and place every day. The unity of the life, like the unity of a regiment's life, was its real quality ; its scattered and diversified air was its superficial aspect.

She told him, now, that they were to have three new " moguls " and a couple of new " hogs " on her division, and asked him, in a detached way, if he was likely to be affected by the change in the boundary of the division at present ending at Maverick. Engineer Demarz had been transferred from engine 210 to 403, as one of

the consequences of the change; Cockleman
was running 210 now, and Vigart was firing for
him. William Masten, Mark Kites, and Fred
Decker were to be the "hostlers" at Maverick.
The round-house foreman at Portre's Junction
was to be married next week. How did Dave
like Hammet to get ahead of him like that?
Had he met the California horse-special that
went through yesterday to take the trotters on
to the Eastern race-meetings? The smelter at
Rexiana had shut down, and the road wasn't
hauling any more ore there; the coal-field at
Cannel was sending through thirty cartloads a
day, though. The boys said there was to be
a new time-table out in a fortnight; but she
didn't believe it would affect him, anyway.

"Look out there," shouted Dave, as she
stepped out gaily on the railway bridge. "Let
me go first." The river which ran through the
cañon took its course here through a deep gorge,
a hundred feet below the level of the track. The
bridge spanning it was of wood, and a single

24

plank was laid loosely over the ties, between the rails, for the use of track-walkers. The crossing of the bridge by this plank was a dizzying business, requiring experience and a cool head. Reffey, who had been brought up in a prairie country, had never seen such a bridge until two months before, and she had been accustomed to let Dave go ahead and give her a guiding or supporting hand where she needed it. But she was in a mood to-day to make him wince under her power, and perversely, at the same time, in a mood of humbleness and frankness which made her wish to show herself to him as she really was.

"Pooh!" she cried, looking back at him over her shoulder, as she balanced on the plank above the gorge, in a way that turned Dave pale. "Think because you run trains over this bridge you've got to run me over too? *I'm* the conductor of this train."

She moved out a dozen steps further, taking care how she put down her foot, as indeed she must, but giving an effect of recklessness to her motions that made Dave sick with fear. He started to follow her out upon the plank ; but she screamed peremptorily :

"Stay where you are till I say you may come. Don't you move, Dave Lewis."

"You're mad, Reffey ! you're mad ! Wait till I can get to you." He made another movement to set forth towards her, but she shouted :

"If you take another step before I tell you I'll go out on the ties."

She made as if to suit the action to the word, and Dave's tongue hung limp in his mouth as he managed to cry back hoarsely, "All right, I won't."

He stood regarding her slow, balancing motions with horror. He had advanced some paces on the plank himself, and when he let his eyes drop he saw the river gleaming between the ties, a hundred feet beneath. Out there, under the spot where Reffey stood, the stream

26

tossed and whitened over a scattered mass of rocks. She was not looking down ; her head was up, her arms out, her eyes straight before her, and she was feeling for the plank with her feet. His heart melted in his breast as he gazed after her.

Suddenly he saw her stoop, as she passed the water-barrel placed on wooden bridges as a precaution against fire. She crept out upon the platform on which the barrel stood, and, gathering her skirts under her, sat down at the edge of it, dangling her feet above the river. Then she looked around at him calmly, and called out :

"You can come now."

Dave drew a long breath, and ran out toward her on the plank. Long use had made the feat easy to him, and he was quickly at her side.

" Well, I'll be—— ! " he said, standing above her.

She looked about at him with a challenging smile.

27

"Don't be. It's more fun out here.

"You're a wicked girl."

"Yes, I know that," she answered, contemplating the toe of her boot, as she swung it out over the abyss. "Did I worry you?" she asked.

"You killed me. I wouldn't go through what you just made me go through, again, for a thousand dollars."

"Well, I won't charge you that. Won't you be seated?"

She mimicked the parlour manner in a niminy-primini voice, and drew in her skirts to give him room on the platform. He sank down beside her, and seized her hand fast in his.

"Promise never to do it again," he demanded huskily in her ear.

She gave a little squeal of pain.

"Le' go my hand."

"Promise."

She looked into his eyes. "All right, Dave; I promise."

28

"And you'll never do it again?"

"Never. Not the same thing. I'm tired of that." He gave her a look of deep reproach, before which she lowered her eyes.

"Oh, Dave!" she murmured, as she cuddled her head on his breast; "I *am* wicked. You don't figure enough on that. It was partly to show you how wicked I am that I did it."

The need for a faith on his part answering to her utter faith in him caused her, at times, to test his belief in her wilfully. She had told him scores of things about herself in the fear that he would find them out and cease to believe in her. She was accustomed to heap up the tale of her proud, passionate, selfish, jealous nature in the nervous longing to make sure of his love, once for all, by exhausting in advance the possibilities of accusation.

They sat silent for a moment after this, while Dave took her to him, and they kissed in a long, reconciling embrace.

"You don't know me, Dave Lewis," she said,

"and I don't suppose you ever will till I make you hate me by doing something that'll hurt you so bad that you'll never have anything more to do with me. It'll be something I can't help doing ; and I'll love you all the same—oh, yes, I'll love you fast enough—but I'll have to do it. And then I'll spend the rest of my life wishing I hadn't. I've got a regular black heart, Dave— that's what I have ; and the sooner you know it, the better."

Dave laughed easily. "I always take mine black," he said.

She patted his hand as she looked up at him. "Well, I only hope you always will."

"I know what you are thinking of," he said.

She enveloped him in the sultry atmosphere of one of her rich glances. "I'll bet you don't," she answered with her head up.

"You're thinking of Mattie—you're thinking we didn't do right by her. I often think that myself."

"*Do* you, Dave Lewis? That little meek,

30

chalk-faced hussy. . . . . Well, then, *I* don't. Do you hear that? *I* don't. I hate her, I do. Understand? I hate her. I'd like to take a dozen men from her, one after the other, and toss her their old hats for keepsakes. I'd like to have her out here where we're sitting—that's all."

"Great Scott, Reffey! You ought to want to be good to her. We've done her harm enough. Anyway, *I* have. If I knew a thing to do for her that wouldn't hurt her worse'n leaving her alone, I'd do it *too* quick."

"Look here, Dave Lewis, if you want to go back to her, you've got an easy chance. Just take that plank and march back to the hotel. You'll find her in the telegraph-office, and glad to see you I shouldn't wonder."

"I ain't hankering to go back to her," he said, sulkily.

"Well, then!" ejaculated Reffey, decisively.

"You don't expect a man to play a trick like that on a woman and *like* it, I hope."

" Don't I, though ? Depends a little on who
he plays it on, and who he does it for, I should
say ! If it were some girls I know and some
men, I should think they'd just go wallowing
around it. I only wish it had been my chance
to give her the mitten. I'd have worked some
prickles into it."

" What a girl you are !" exclaimed Dave. He
said it admiringly, though he had intended to
say it upbraidingly.

"Well, I told you I wasn't good. I ain't. I
better tell you the kind of girl I am, I guess.
You know I come from Topeka, but you don't
know how I come to be there, nor what it was
that drove me into the business. I ain't an eating-house manager by profession. My father—
my own father—kept a store in Kansas City. He
used to speculate in land. We was rich once,
like other people. But the bottom dropped out
of land in Kansas City, my father died, and my
mother married again. My new father lived at
Wichita. He had more education than my

own father, but less brains. First we didn't like each other, and then we hated each other like mad ; but I used to work for him like as if I'd loved him. I got up every morning at four o'clock to get his breakfast and send him off to his machine-shop (mother wasn't much good those days) ; and he was always rowing me about my cooking. The cooking was all right, if I do say it. That wasn't the trouble. He's one of these kind of men that'd find fault with the Garden of Eden if the sun was under a cloud, and the next day'd be praising Sunday-school picnic lemonade. You *couldn't* please him ! Well, one morning I was frying some bacon for him in the kitchen, because he'd said the day before that if there was one thing he did like it was bacon, and I never give it to him. He came out into the kitchen, where I was heating myself up over the stove for him— and first he didn't like bacon, never eat it, and never would eat it ; and then he began to criticise around about the way I was frying it.

C

That got my blood up, but I didn't say nothing; then he went sniffing at it, and bending over to look at it close, and telling me to turn it this way and that, and showing me how he wanted it cooked, till I was ready to fly out of my skin. And I *told* him! Says I, 'Look here; you *know* I got a notorious temper. I ain't got no control of myself if you rouse me. Just take warning now, Jim Phelan (that's what I always called him), or it'll be the worse for you.'

" He just smiled at me and went on, and then I up with the whole boiling skillet of fat and grease and let him have it. It took him full in the face, and he dropped into a chair as if he'd been shot, howling with the pain like a wild animal, and I just looked at him and asked him, 'Well? How do you like it?' I didn't have no more bacon to cook, and I could give my entire attention to him. He shrieked for a doctor (mother wasn't to home that day), and I smiled at him. Then he knelt down on the kitchen floor, with that grease dripping all down

34

his face and out of his beard (you don't know how funny he looked), and regularly prayed me to do something for him. But I told him I wasn't running for doctors so much this week as I was last, and it did me good all through. Well, then I ran away, of course, and went to Topeka, and got a place as dining-room girl. After six months or so they found I could run girls, and they made me head-waitress. You just see what I am, Dave. I ain't good. I love my friends and hate my enemies; and when it comes into my head to do a thing I do it, and if I'm mad I'll do anything. Sometimes I don't think a girl like me is going to bring you happiness, Dave. But then I remember how I love you, and after that I think of some one else having you, and——" She bit her white little teeth together. "Well, about that time I'm willing to make you miserable."

Dave refused the prospect of wretchedness she offered him, of course, and denied her capacity to furnish it. He said how she was

35

his life, his happiness, and his only hope ; and said it, as they sat on their dizzy perch, with a thousand circumstances of endearment. The narrow mountain torrent chafed against its walls down there at the bottom of the gorge, further beneath them than Reffey really liked to make sure of with her eyes. It tormented itself upon the rocks with moans and eery cries ; it split and bubbled in showers of spray, and raced on to a crashing death over the fall in sight from the bridge. The crags rose on either side of their resting-place into pinnacles that hid the sun and made an early twilight in the cañon.

II.

MEANWHILE Mattie sat in her little telegraph and ticket office, " visiting " with Kate Farley, the operator at Red Rock, the station at the other end of the cañon. They held conversations like this over the wire daily, during slack hours after the day's markets had been sent through, and when the line was not much in use for commercial work. Their acquaintance had begun with an inquiry from Kate about the geraniums in Mattie's window. She telegraphed her that her "steady," Milton Drew (who had just been promoted from his position as fireman of 192 to that of engineer of 308), had noticed them blooming in her window on his journeys back and forth, and had twitted her on the poor show hers made beside those in the office at Mitcham's. Kate wanted to know how Mattie made hers grow, and Mattie, who was the most good-natured person possible, had told her. They knew all about each other's affairs now, and were bosom friends, though they had never met.

They even described their offices to each other; and Kate knew that Mattie had her walls papered with cuttings from *The Illustrated London News*, left by one of the English visitors to the Hotel (Kate's walls were covered with fashion-plates); that there was a rag-carpet on the floor, a "busy bee" clock on the shelf, a bear-skin under Mattie's feet, and by her side a window-box covered with a piece from one of her mother's trousseau dresses. She also knew that her chief possession was a dog, an Irish setter, which she kept constantly by her   Kate pictured the little room as the neat, quiet, domestic spot it was; and rightly imagined it as like Mattie.

It was to Kate, as her nearest friend, that Mattie had first told the news of her engagement to Dave, and Kate had telegraphed back a hug, and a rattle of applause not in the Morse alphabet.   Then she had fired questions at Mattie, who had ticked back her answers with shy jerkiness.   She told her friend that Dave was the best and dearest fellow in the world, and Kate had shown her teeth from Red Rock, and laughed back that she supposed as much. Kate made Mattie give her daily news of the progress of the affair after this; it superseded their geraniums as a theme of conversation, and

38

Mattie bore Kate's electrical digs and gibes
without attempting retaliation in kind.   Kate
wasn't at all shy about Milt, which made all the
difference; and, indeed, Mattie liked the subject
of Dave too well to grudge the expense of
teasing for the right to talk him over.   They
talked almost as much of clothes as of Dave, for
Mattie was doing in the office her own sewing
for the wedding, and she could ask Kate's
advice at the end of any seam by reaching out
her hand.   When the trains came in, she put
her tell-tale needlework carefully away, wrapped
(with her dreams) in the fair linen cloth she
kept for the purpose; stood up in her little box,
raised the rolling front of her ticket-rack, slid
up the window separating her from the prose of
the outer world, and was a woman of affairs
again.

She stamped tickets with a business-like
bang of her little fist, and rattled off train-
messages, and received orders and reports, as
if nothing of the Dave kind or of the love kind

existed on the planet. When the train was
Dave's, and he leaned over her counter to sign
his name in the train-book, a perception of facts
of this order certainly got into her eyes ; but
this was all she allowed herself in business
hours. On Dave's day off, when he came over
from Portoe's Junction, he loafed about her
office, watching her movements affectionately
while she attended to her duties, and made
plans with her, when she was not busy, for the
time after their marriage. When No. 3 had
passed (Dave's train every other day) Mattie's
time became her own, and it was their custom
to take long evening walks in the cañon or
among the hills. On the nights when their
walks led them into the black and awful beauty
of the cañon Mattie liked Dave to pilot her over
the bridge, though her mountain-bred step was
surer than his railway-man's nimbleness. The
moon, rising late for wayfarers in depths a
thousand feet below the world that saw its first
beams, would often discover a pair of lovers, far

down in that rocky dimness, whispering to each other. These were sweet evenings to Mattie, and, until Reffey came, they were not less dear to Dave.

When he threw her over she seemed at first like one mortally stricken. Afterward she roused herself and went on, in order to rightly hate Reffey. It was the woman who had taken him from her whom she blamed, of course; Dave could never have turned false if she had left him his senses. She had bewitched him, and the fault was no more his than if a serpent had fixed a fatal eye on him. The deep forces of a still, temperate nature were alive in Mattie now; she had not the habit of valuing herself, nor of regarding herself as entitled to things, and she had almost no aggression, but Reffey had roused a tiger in her. She daily found new ways of hating her and new reasons for hating her. Reffey's assured and familiar air with Dave, as if it were to her that he had been long engaged, the easy impudence with which she had accomplished her theft, even the perception that Reffey would have borne the hurt much better if it had fallen to her lot, sharpened her rancour. She fancied, with gnashing teeth, how cleverly Reffey would have made a triumph of being jilted, so that every one would think it precisely what she had all along been desiring ; she saw Reffey showing herself gaily the next day at an engineer's ball or a firemen's excursion with a defying face and a rollicking smile for the boys ; and Mattie loathed herself for not being strong enough for this, though she had no heart to answer back, so far as Dave was concerned, nor any real wish to shine with this impossible address. Toward Dave no pride, nor savageness of stolidity, nor mere concealment, nor any other maidenly defence came to her aid ; the wound he had dealt remained open and palpable to him ; if he looked her way he could not fail to see his work, and perhaps this touched him more than any hardness could have done.

42

She suffered to herself; her mother was long dead; Mitcham's was her only home, and, unless she excepted Kate, she had no friends. The difficulty of telling Kate was finally the cruelest measure of his cruelty; for a week she continued to answer questions about her dresses, and even about him, with a breaking heart. She simply had not the courage to tell her; and when she brought herself to it at last, Kate wired back furiously that she wasn't "sending" decently; how did she expect her to "take" from such work, especially when what she seemed to be trying to tell her was so interesting? Then certain male operators on the line, who made daily bets with each other on the "game," and who wanted to talk over the drubbing Chicago had given New York (they had not let them get a run), cut in to ask if thos girls were going to gabble *all* day; and Mattie gave it up.

Mattie watched Dave hanging on Reffey's words as he had been used to hang on hers,

43

gazing into her eyes with the fond smile that
had once belonged to her alone, using the thousand little tricks of affection that had once
seemed invented for her (poor fool !) and con-
secrated to her; and she saw Reffey bloom
under these stolen blessings. It was hard to
see them together, but much harder when she
did not see them, and her fancy was left to gnaw
bitterly upon itself. Their walks in the cañon,
or among the hills, brought tortures with them
that seemed, each time, to leave a permanent
mark on her spirit. To-day she had watched
them from her window leave the hotel arm in
arm, then separate, and step from tie to tie, dis-
appearing in the direction of the bridge. She
knew from the wires that a "special" was on its
way over the range, bearing certain Eastern
railway officials in their private car ; and she
knew that Dave and Reffey did not know it,
and supposed the last train to have passed,
until the hour when the evening express was
due. She followed them with gleaming eyes ;

44

it wasn't her business to tell them. Dave was able to look after his new lady-love for himself, she supposed. They might meet the train in a part of the cañon where there was room, like as not ; and if it came around a curve before they knew, or caught them on the bridge, they'd enjoy dying in each other's arms. It wasn't her lookout. They didn't ask advice from her about their walks ; they hadn't invited her to follow them.

"Three's a crowd !" whispered Mattie to herself, pressing her face against the pane.

She would be a murderer. . . . . What ? Sitting in her office, looking out of the window ? That was a good joke.

But she would.

"Who's doing anything ?" muttered Mattie to the window.

Kissing and spooning—they were having a good time in there between the cañon walls. Better not interrupt them !

The thought of Dave came over her smother-

45

ingly; she gasped. It was not her Dave, nor
Reffey's Dave—merely Dave. She loved him.
She could not let him die like that. She threw
a shawl over her head and laid a hand on the
knob of the office-door. Then she stopped.
Could she save them for each other? Could
she bear to see them happy later, and know it
to be through her? If they died together—
they wouldn't; it was crazy to think that a
railroad-man, and a clever fellow like Dave,
wouldn't have more hustle about him than that,
but if they did, it blotted out her trouble; it
stopped the pain in her breast. She needn't
turn the knob. Her hold relaxed. The grim
thought that followed made her tighten it
again; she turned the knob and went out and
down the track. What had come to her was
that Dave would *not* be happy with Reffey—no,
never in this world—and that, if she wanted her
revenge on both of them, she would save them
to marry each other. When she came to the
bridge and saw them seated there in the

affectionate attitude already described, she halted, and had almost turned back ; but her thought came to her again ; and she called out sullenly, from the edge of the gorge :

" Better come off there ! "

They looked up at the sound, and together saw the little figure on the bank of the river—a small pale face framed in a tightly drawn shawl, which fell down the straight lines of an almost tiny form.   Her dog was standing by her side.

They recognised her together, and Reffey gave a shrill laugh.   Dave laid a hand on her arm for silence.

" What's the matter ? " he called back to Mattie.

" *Special !* "

" The devil !   Get up, Reffey. "

" Don't I look like it ? "

" You look like a mad woman.   Do you want to be killed out here ? "

Reffey made her rosy mouth into a point.

47

"I don't want to be saved—not by her," she said swinging her legs.

"Good heavens ! what *do* you want ? "

"This suits me pretty well," she said, glancing up at him, with a tantalising smile.

"Come, no fooling !   There's a train coming, I tell you ! "

"Well, get out of the way of it, then."

"Do you suppose I'm going without you ?"

No answer.

"Look here, Reffey Deacon, get up off there and come along with me, or I'll carry you."

"I wouldn't do that," she responded quietly.

"Why not ?" asked Dave, stupefied.

"I'll jump."

Dave uttered a raging oath, and looked about him helplessly.

"Well, say what you *do* want me to do then, and say it quick."

"Get out of the way of the train, I tell you, if it's coming.   Go over to your friend there.   I'll take care of myself."

48

"You'll be killed."

Reffey pushed out her lower lip quickly, and dropped her eyes.

Dave laid a hand on her shoulder ; she looked around at him.

" If I go, will you save yourself?"

" That's *just* what I'll do," she said, pursing her lips and nodding her head. " I don't have to ask Mattie Baker to do it for me." And, after a pause, " Nor you either, Dave Lewis, when she sets you on ! "

"Well, I'll be——! " began her lover.

She turned and nodded at him. "Good-bye ! " " Oh, good-bye ! " shouted Dave, turning on his heel, and going swiftly toward Mattie.

At the same moment Reffey got deliberately upon her feet, slipped out to the central plank, holding on by the barrel, and turning her back upon him and upon Mattie, began a progress to the other bank best described as a saunter.

In building the bridge and making the curve

in the track, on the bank opposite that on which Mattie stood, a deep hollow had been excavated in the face of the rock. Reffey had noted it from her seat above the river. She stepped off the bridge and tucked herself into it, as the special roared by her, darted out upon the bridge, and swept by Dave and Mattie, on the other side. The wind it made caught her dress as she crouched back in her shelter, and blew it tight about her. She held her big hat on with one hand, and looked across the chasm to see the negro porter waving a greeting to her from the rear platform of the last car, and to catch sight of Dave, standing on the opposite bank talking earnestly to Mattie, who was turning away.

He was thanking her with embarrassment, or trying to say how they could never thank her enough. If Reffey could have heard him including her in the obligation, she would not have remained under the shadow of the rock until they parted.

50

Mattie was saying, with lowered eyes, " I guess you don't want to be very thankful to me, Mr. Lewis, and I guess I don't want to have you."

" Of course. You hate me. *I* know that. It's only natural."

Mattie shook her head and rubbed the gravel backward and forward with her foot. " No, Mr. Lewis, I don't hate you."

"Well, then, it's because you're too good. I've given you cause enough, Heaven knows. Mattie, I've been wanting this long time to tell you—only, somehow, I never got the chance— that I don't think any more of myself than you do ; not a bit ; I had to ; I wasn't responsible. I can say that ; and it's the best I *can* say. But it don't excuse me any."

"There ain't any need of excuses as I know of," responded Mattie, with dignity.

"Well, then, there ought to be. If a woman had treated me the way I've treated you, I wouldn't think *excuses* was in it—much !

You're a first-class, nickel-plated angel, Mattie ; that's what you are ! "

Mattie shut one lip upon the other. " I guess I rather get what praise I *do* get somewheres else, Mr. Lewis," she said quietly.

"All right. But I'll never get over what I done to you, Mattie. I want you should know that—never ! If it's any comfort, you can know that what I did ain't always such a comfort as it might be."

Mattie looked up, with a spark in her eye. "You mean—*her?*"

"Well, I was thinking how it hurt me all the time to remember 'bout you."

"You needn't," interposed Mattie, for very shame, though the pretence of a hardihood in which she knew he couldn't believe (how could he, when he knew her, when he had made her tell him a thousand times how she loved him?) did not give her the smallest pleasure.

" But perhaps it ain't so far from true of the

52

other either," Dave pursued thoughtfully. He had not even heard her protest.

Mattie drew her shawl together as if to leave him. She looked into his eyes a moment.

" You ain't going to be happy, Dave."

"You mean I oughtn't to be after what I've done?"

"I mean you ain't going to be," repeated Mattie doggedly; and with this she turned and left him.

Next morning she received, through the usual channel, a communication from Kate; and when Reffey knocked at the window of her ticket-office, in the course of the morning, Mattie raised it, and met her with a new look in her eyes.

"The less we have to say to each other the better," Reffey began from outside, immediately the window was raised; "but I just come to say you needn't do that again. *I'd* rather stay and take my chances with the cow-catcher twenty times over."

53

Mattie surveyed her for a moment and they exchanged glances of cold repugnance.

"I ain't very likely to," said Mattie at last, measuring Reffey scornfully.

The manager of the eating-house was looking offensively well—tall, commanding, buxom, rich-coloured, satisfied, prosperous. Mattie looked out at her from the other side of the window, conscious of her own pinched face, haggard with weeping and with wakeful nights, and a burning throb of jealousy went through her. All that fairness, and health, and well-being seemed stolen from her, too, as her lover had been stolen. A frenzy of loathing seized her, and the news that had saddened her half an hour before rejoiced her now with the hope of bruising that haughty happiness with it.

"Well, see you don't; that's all," rejoined Reffey. "I can get along, I guess, without being beholden to *you* for my life, and so can Dave. Oh, I know what you did it for !'

"I didn't do it for you."

54

"You didn't get the chance. *I* was ready for you."

"Nor for him, either," continued Mattie, without raising her voice.

"What then, please?" demanded Reffey, briskly.

"I didn't want either of you to get killed," pursued Mattie steadily. "I wanted you to live."

"*Did* you?"

"To marry each other," Mattie went on quietly. "You're going to marry a thief; did you know that?"

Reffey blew an amused, derisive sound between her lips, glancing carelessly down at Mattie from her superior height.

"Yes, you're going to marry a thief. Heaven won't let such things be as you've done and nothing to pay. Be sure of that, Rebecca Deacon! You've swindled me out of Dave, but you can't swindle the powers above. Your house is being built with stolen money."

Reffey's face went quickly to a ghastly pallor. " Who says it ? Who dares ?"

" *I* do. Do you want any one worse to know it than me. I guess I enjoy it as much as most any one would. You didn't rob me of such a prize *after* all, did you, Miss Deacon ? "

Reffey's face grew whiter, and then an unwholesome dusky blue. Rage choked her. She thrust her arms quickly through the ticket-window, seized Mattie by her narrow little shoulders, and shook her viciously.

" Aw, you——" she stammered, breathlessly with passion. " You——" But she could not piece another word to it.

Mattie wriggled out of her strong grasp, and retreated against the corrugated black-walnut roller of her ticket-rack.

" That's all right," she said, gasping, but still quietly. " But he's knocking down fares every day, all the same, and you'll live in a house that's built with them."

Reffey leaned through the window with blazing eyes, and hurled these words at her:

"Don't think it! Hear! *Don't—you—think—it!* You're a liar, Mattie Baker; but if you weren't, and lived in hopes of *that* sweet sight to comfort your sore eyes, you'd be the most almightily left little girl between here and Salt Lake. *I'm* on in this scene. See! I'm right here, and that ain't my sort. Cast off! . . . ." she ended between her teeth, in an indescribable fury of scorn and malice. Then she went.

III.

SIX weeks later Reffey and Dave were married. She had not questioned him; not only because she wouldn't do Mattie so much honour, but because she didn't believe it, and if she did, Dave was too clever to be found out, so that it wouldn't be true, anyway. As to whether Dave was actually a thief or not, she cared practically nothing; and besides, what he was doing, *if* he was doing it (which he wasn't), was not thieving. It was—well, it was "knocking down," which was nothing out of the way unless discovered. *Then* it was stealing fast enough ; but she didn't take herself for fool enough to be in love with a man who would do such a thing, *and* be found out. Hardly !

They were married in the dining-room at Mitcham's by a clergyman whom Dave deadheaded over from Portoe's Junction. All the dining-room girls were there, and the new eating-house manager, who had been transferred from Maverick to take Reffey's place ; so were all the men on Dave's division who could get off. Reffey looked as beautiful and sumptuous and perfect in her bridal dress as Dave could have wished or fancied ; and he quieted the accusing pang of memory, as he looked about him and saw that Mattie wasn't there, with his deep satisfaction in the situation as it stood. He beamed on all his friends, in fact, as became a bridegroom, and no one who looked at his

58

cheerful face could have supposed that a corner of his breast was given over to a heavy and dispiriting remorse. Mattie's words mixed themselves hideously with the words of the marriage service. "You ain't going to be happy, Dave," the clergyman seemed to be saying : Dave was uncertain in the responses.

The "collation," which Reffey had prepared with her own hands, kept them, with other festival matters, until No. 3 stood at their door, like a bridal chariot, waiting to speed them over to Maverick. They had the compartment in the Pullman to themselves, of course ; and it was one of the brakemen who got on the roof, while the crowd was shouting farewells on the eating-house platform, and shied rice at them through the ventilator.

They were not going to take a wedding journey, unless the trip over the range to Maverick could count for that. Dave couldn't well get off for a long enough time to make it worth while.

Jake Riker, the station hackman whom Dave
had been accustomed to employ for his hasty
conferences with his builder, was waiting for
them on the platform at Maverick by Dave's
orders. The newly made husband gave the
order to drive to the house he had prepared for
Reffey with a nervous twitch in his voice ; he
was taking his wife home—the word sent a
pleasant tingle through him—but would she
like what he had done for her ? He knew by
this time Reffey's capacity for not liking things.
Suppose she shouldn't like this ? Suppose it
should all prove useless — the affectionate
planning, the solicitous overseeing, the choosing
and buying and thought and work ? As they
were whirled along toward the house, and
Reffey's hand lay moist in his, he remembered
hours stolen from sleep to get half a day at
Maverick for a talk with his builder, and the
weary days at Denver with furniture-men and
carpet-dealers and paper-hangers, and the
prospect of a disappointment for Reffey at the

end of it all, disheartened him. If she would
only like it, how little he should grudge his
pains! The notion of "surprising" her with it
all, which had possessed so rich an interest for
him, now seemed silly. It was only by remind-
ing himself that, in any event, she couldn't have
left her work at Mitcham's long enough to
advise at Maverick or Denver that he got up
the cheerfulness to leap from the carriage when
they drew up before the house, to throw open
the front door for her, and then, as she came up
the walk to him, to lift her over the threshold
with a bouncing swing and to welcome her,
within, gaily.

She gave him his kiss when the hack had
driven away, the door was shut behind them, and
they stood in their little parlour, alone with each
other. It was a fierce, devouring kiss, claiming
him and making him hers, and hers only, for all
and for ever. She clutched him to her tight,
possessing him with a savage tenderness; she
put back his head to gaze into his eyes; her own

swam in a soft languor. Then she rumpled his hair over his forehead, making inarticulate murmurs of love ; she kissed him again once, twice, and then very many times.

"Oh, darling, darling, dear darling, I love you !" she whispered. "Did you know that ? I love you."

Dave caught her to him rapturously, and then held her away, and let his eyes feed long on her brilliant, ardent beauty. The adoring face, in which she let him read for the first time all her love, was dizzying, blinding. He snatched his gaze from it.

"You haven't looked at the room yet ?" he said.

" Haven't I ?" she returned dreamily, cradling herself in his arms.

" No."

" Well ?" cooed she contentedly.

" Oh, well, there's plenty of time."

"Lots. Only think—we're going to live here."

" Yes—together."

"Together !" she murmured.

A long pause fell.

"Well, I suppose I may as well," she said at last, with a deep sigh.

"What ?"

"See what you've been doing for me, you old goose." She gave his cheek a playful cuff, and turned to survey the room, taking off her bonnet as she did so, and laying it on the sofa. Dave watched her in pain and doubt.

"Oh, Dave !" she exclaimed.

"Yes. What ?"

"You *dear!* You Jim Dandy ! You out and outer !"

He laughed in uneasy relief. "I did as well as I knew how, without you."

She heaved a deep breath. "W-e-l-l !" she said, spreading the monosyllable out to the thinness of ecstasy, "it's my size !"

Dave trembled with happiness, and he let her kiss him in stupid unresponse.

She darted away from him to the couch she saw over his shoulder.

"So you went and got the white and gold and thin legs after all?"

"Yes."

She stamped her foot on the red Persian rug, letting her shoe sink confirmatorily into its thick pile.

"And this?" Dave nodded. She gave a little shiver of luxury as she cast an inclusive glance round the room, and said, "If you ask *me*, Dave Lewis, *I* believe you've bought all the things you told me you couldn't afford."

Dave laughed. "Shouldn't wonder."

"Well, you're a beaut' from Lovelyville, David, and I don't care who knows it."

"Better see the rest of the house before you make too sure. Come on upstairs."

He lighted the huge parlour-lamp, with its duplex burner and immense red shade, and she followed him. There were plenty of smaller amps in the house, but he had a fancy that some e

64

of the things he had bought would look best through red, and, at all events, he wanted to show her the lamp at once. It had an immediate success with her ; she praised it all the way upstairs, where, however, further examples of her husband's lavishness and taste won away her applause. She went about hanging on his arm and patting it softly, with whispers of delight and gurgles of gratitude and pleasure, as he held the lamp aloft in his other hand, flashing it into rooms which they presently visited, illuminating corners and closets, and turning it on objects which he had bought expressly in the hope that she would like them. She always liked them, she liked everything, and Dave, his fears put to shame, was ready to break his red shade in embracing her.

Returned to the ground floor, he ushered her into the dining-room, which she greeted with a shout of approval.

She tossed her chin teasingly at him. " Laid yourself out on that buffet, didn't you ?" It was a monstrous black walnut structure, over which thick varnished bunches of machine carving were plastered ; the top was of an ugly red marble ; the wood-work terminated above the mirror in a point, on which a seedy angel pirouetted.

Dave grunted serenely. He had got beyond the articulate expressions of gratification. Reffey went up to the imposing piece of furniture and drew her hand reverently over the marble. After a moment she stooped to look at herself in the mirror, smoothing her hair.

"Well ; I've served things from buffets like that," she exclaimed, "and I've worked for people that owned them ; but I never thought to have one for my very own."

She opened the doors below the marble, and peered in at the shelves; she espied the silver and dragged it out and sprawled it on the table, rummaging it lovingly over under her hands. "Roll plate !" she said, under her breath, " twelve table, two dozen tea, and—yes, a dozen

dessert. Oh, I've always wanted dessert!"
She sprang on him, and gave him such a hug
as he would never have dared to picture in his
reveries.

"Well," she said immediately, as she pushed
him off to regard him properly, "you *have* done
it!"

"I don't know as I've spared money," said
Dave modestly.

She looked fondly at him. "You've spent
it through a hose, David. Come into the
kitchen."

The kitchen also seemed good to her—better,
if possible, than the things that had gone before.
It appealed to her on the professional side : she
saw opportunities in the shining rows of fresh
tins, the blue enamelled ware, the pots and pans.
She turned them over skilfully, and sounded
them with her knuckles, and lifted a lid from
the cooking-stove, and sniffed at the sink. Then
she took his arm and drew him into the parlour,
and made him sit in the wicker chair before the

fire, where he had always planted her in fancy, and, for herself, dropped on the floor, and leaned an arm on his knee, while she looked up at him in a rapture of content.

The fire of piñon logs blazing in the grate cast a ruddy glow upon her face, out of which the sinister lines seemed for the moment purified. She took a newspaper from the table, in idleness, and glanced up and down its columns with the indulgent glance women give newspapers. It was a copy of the Maverick *Sentinel*.

"Have you subscribed, Dave?"

"Yes; I thought it 'ud make us feel sort of home-like to find a paper in the house, as if we'd always lived here."

"You sweetums! You've thought of everything. I wonder if every girl is so lucky.' She mused a moment, as her eyes returned to the paper. "They've got a railroad column, haven't they?" she commented, pointing to a series of items headed " Track and Round-House Cinders," and surmounted by a cut of a locomotive.

"Yes; that's the advantage of living at the end of the division. We'll get all the news."

"That's the kind," said Reffey approvingly. "Why, here's your name!" She started up. "But *Dave*—— !"

"Well? They got a grind on me about the ceremony? Preacher, county clerk, and furnished house for two? I supposed as much."

Something in her averted face startled him. "Why, what's the matter, Reffey?" He forced her to turn toward him, and she faced him with a gaze of reproach and bitterness that searched his soul. He snatched up the paper and read for himself:

"Dave Lewis, the popular conductor of Nos. 3 and 14, has got the grand bounce from headquarters, we understand. Moving cause, the good old custom of 'knocking down.' As he has just led to the altar Miss Reffey Deacon, of Mitcham's, well and favourably known as the manager of the railroad eating-house at that place, the g.b. comes at a bad time for the happy pair."

" Oh, *Dave!* "

He looked up and encountered Reffey's hard eye, still fixed on him.

" Don't look that way, Reffey. What's the dif.? They all do it."

" I know that," answered she hoarsely. "But the rest don't get found out !"

He turned from her accusing and scornful gaze. " I suppose you're afraid I can't get another situation. You needn't be. I've got a place offered me on another road ; I've had it this long time. I'll take that."

" Oh, I ain't worrying about you none. Don't you fret. Where's my bonnet?" She turned and found it on the sofa where she had left it, and clapped it on her head, adjusting it with a vigorous movement, and jamming in the long pins in her haste as she could.

" Where are you going?"

70

"Out of this house."

"Don't be a fool !"

"Well, I'm going to try hard not to be, Dave Lewis." She gave him a quick look. "You coming?"

"Didn't know as I was invited," he responded with a ghastly effort at gaiety.

"Well, you are. 'Tain't *you* I'm running away from."

He dropped the paper and stared at her. "What then?"

"This house."

"*What !*"

"That's what I said," returned Reffey coldly, drawing her wrap over her shoulders.

"Why?"

She shut her lips. "Mattie Baker."

"See here, Reffey Lewis, are you a rip-roaring maniac, or a sensible woman and my wife?"

Reffey came and stood before him, with blazing eyes.

"Do you think I could live an hour in a house that Mattie Baker could say was built with knock-downs?"

The ferocious pride and malignity of her tone beat him down. He could not lay his tongue to a word.

"How do I know?" he said at last, sulkily.

"Well, then, put on your hat."

"Now look here——!" he began with renewed anger as he found himself.

"Don't I tell you I can hear her saying it? I ain't responsible for myself just about now, I give you notice, Dave Lewis. Come on!"

He restrained an inclination to clasp his hands about her fair throat and draw them tighter, till she begged for mercy.

"What kind of woman are you, anyway?" he cried in rage, as she gathered the strings within her cloak and caught them about her waist, where she tied them with a vicious jerk.

72

" The kind that don't take a man from another woman and then give her the chance to say she's better off without him than I am with him. The kind that don't give any living mortal a whip over her—the kind that 'ud kill herself with a smile before she give it to Mattie Baker. The sort that *hates*, if you want to know!"

She was drawing on her gloves rapidly. Dave regarded her in helpless admiration and fascination as she gave vent to this astounding outburst. She *was* the only one off her piece of goods!

"I know that Reffey! I know it," he said soothingly. "But you ain't going to leave our house on our wedding-night—the house I've built and furnished for you, the house I've worked so to please you with. You don't know what it's cost me—the work and the money! *Our* house, Reffey! Ours, however it come! Ours! That sounds pretty good to me; I don't know how it does to you."

73

He stooped over her shoulder and tried to kiss her, but she pushed him off.

"Ours! Not much it ain't! A house that any one can point at and nudge the person with him, and smile, and say 'Pretty tidy house that —know how it was built, I suppose?' A house that Mattie Baker'll know *that's* happening to every day! Ours! It's hers, I tell you—*hers!* *I* don't belong to her to pity, though—not yet! Come along if you're coming!"

She strode from the room, and Dave could only follow her. She waited at the gate while he locked the door; then they walked on together in silence toward the railroad from which they had come an hour before. A full moon shone down on them out of the fathomless, steely blue of these altitudes, blanching the snowy hills behind them to the whiteness of light. It was midnight and the radiance fell upon a silent town—expressing its raw, haphazard outlines with the bareness and cruelty of daylight. The moonshine turned molten on

74

the tin roofs, which grew upon the eye in the similitude of floating vessels of silver. The stillness was broken suddenly by a crash of brass instruments, which cleared itself in a moment into the strains of "He's gone and he's married Yum-Yum"; the sound came from the outskirts of the town. Dave guessed that "The Independent Maverick Brass Band — Sons of Veterans" was on its way to serenade them at the house they had just quitted.

Reffey was pushing hurriedly on with a long, nervous stride; her face was absorbed and white; she had not heard the band. He was about to call her attention to it, when she turned suddenly upon him.

"Lem' me have your key. I've forgotten something."

Her voice was harder than before; but, deep down in it, he thought he detected a sob. Perhaps she was relenting.

"Lem' me take it," she repeated nervously.

75

He handed it to her. "Wait here," she said, and went quickly back to the house.

She put the key in the door, and pushed in to the parlour. The fire was still burning brightly in the grate. With the tongs she snatched it out upon the floor—one log and then another, until they lay, scattered, flaming on the Persian rug. The pile was thick ; the rug did not catch instantly. She went to the window, tore down the lace curtains hanging there and fed them to the flame. Seeing the *Sentinel* still lying on the table, she added it. Then the pile leaped up.

At the door she paused for a last look at the dear room—fresh, lovely, habitable a moment before; now melting into flames before her eyes. She made an instinctive motion forward as if to stop it ; then checked herself proudly, and, without another look behind her, locked the door, and walked back to rejoin Dave.

She gave him the key. "Better go to the hotel, hadn't we ?"

He looked at her curiously. "Yes ; I suppose so."

They went on in silence. As they reached the railway platform, where the hotel stood, Dave looked up, perceiving the light in the sky that was not the light of the moon. He wheeled about and gazed behind him.

"Good God, Reffey ! What's that ?" He clutched her arm.

"The house."

"What ? How do you know ? Who—who did it ?" the poor fellow stammered.

"*I* did," she answered coldly.

He turned a pale, staring, sick face upon her. " *You !* "

" H'm, hum !" nodded Reffey comfortably.

A cold feeling tightened about his heart. The vision of a long life with the woman beside him seemed to stretch away and away into a hopeless blackness.

He gazed at the mounting flame that was swallowing up his work, his love, his happiness, his honesty. The town was alive now ; the shouts came to him ; the gong on the hurrying engine seemed sounding on his soul.

"'You ain't going to be happy, Dave,'" he said to himself, softly.

"What ?"

"Nothing."

MILTON, NEW HAMPSHIRE,
October 3, 1889.

AM thirty-two. I am not married. Yesterday I found a
grey hair. My hair is light ;
it should not begin to turn
so early. I am young. Isn't
thirty-two young ? We don't talk of age together. But of course he knows. I am not
young; I have to remember that. By village
standards, by marriage standards, I am just not
middle-aged ; that is, there is hope for me still.
Oh ! oh ! oh ! for the time when there will no
longer be hope, for the day when they will all
give me up—the mother (dear mother !), the
aunts, my girl friends who have married, the

men who notch off birthdays in their cane-
bottomed chairs in front of the Iroquois
House.

The girl friends are the worst—though there
is always mother. But mother is happy. *Her*
marriage is a success. The marriages of the
girls have been failures in various keys. Mother
came in under the old arrangement. What do I
mean by the old arrangement? I don't know ;
but the arrangement under which Sallie Beaumont was *not* married. Yes ; that's it—the
simple, natural arrangement. You should have
heard Sallie's reason for marrying Fred Maxim ;
they weren't simple, I promise you. Even to a
journal I shouldn't like to tell all those reasons.
When I think that Fred might some day come
to know what they were, I shrivel into a pucker.
I wonder if men would ever dare to marry
women if they could know *all* their reasons for
consenting? Sometimes, perhaps. But none
of the girls whose courtships, and engagements,
and marriages I have watched from my maidenly

watch-tower—my old maidenly watch-tower, I should begin to call it now, I suppose—would like to be called upon to explain to their husbands all that was in their hearts as they went up the aisle on their father's arm. That I know. Perhaps I know too much. I know a great deal too much to make marriage the simple thing for me that it was for mother.

I wish to Gracious that every one wouldn't tell me everything, and I especially wish that I hadn't be n ob iged to go through Sallie Beaumont's engagement with her. Sallie's engagement, do I say? Dear me! Kate Duffie d's, Margaret Hart's, Daisy Monteith's, Helen Everard's, Sadie Macafee's—what of them? It frightens me just to set them down. But it ought to strengthen me to think that I'm here after it all.

Every one has his misfortunes. It has been mine to be the only girl in Milton who has not at some time between her twentieth and thirtieth year been engaged. I don't mean that my not

having been engaged has been a misfortune ;
much the contrary. But my freedom from all
such bother has given me time to look after
the engagements of other girls. At least they
have thought it did. Sallie couldn't have brought
her trouble about Fred Maxim and Jimmy
Dexter (she was in love with Jimmy, and she
knew she ought to marry Fred—Sallie was
always intelligent) to Kate or Daisy. Kate
was trying to think herself into love with Ned
Fellows just then ; and Daisy—but I could
write a novel about Daisy's case. It was this
way : The other girls were busy, and they each
saw that I wasn't—at least not in that way.
Their doubts and their hesitations, and their
woulds and their wouldn'ts, and their final
plunge—well, they were awfully interesting
But they were wearing. I used to go upstairs.
after Sallie had been proposing unanswerable
problems about Fred and Jimmy for an hour in
our parlour, and go to bed. Mother used to
wonder what kept me so miserable. The truth

was, I was suffering sympathetically for those girls. Perhaps you don't know what it is to decide to confide your future to six men at once. I didn't. But I know now. Twelve, I ought to say; for each of the girls had her doubts about some other man. But we declined him; so that really only makes six.

October 4.—I thought I could never keep a journal. I was sure that as soon as I tried to journalise this life I lead it would escape : the things that you can't say (that your hand gets too tired, and ink too shallow, and paper too small, to say) are so many, many more than the things you *can* say. And yet the things that you manage to fix are so interesting that, if you know how to fill up the blanks as I do, you find it fun, on the whole. That is the advantage of writing for your own eye alone : you don't have to fill up the blanks ; and yet when you come to the real point, you can talk it down to bare bones with yourself, without caring for proportion, or perspective, or the relative importance of one of your doings to another. The relative importance of one's doings is just what one thinks it, of course. My last winter's trip to Southern California (it was delightful) would make more of a figure in a biography of me than the way Dick looked at me last evening when he said "Good-night," I suppose; but that only shows the stupidity of biographers. How can they know?—Which brings me to the real point : Why should I care how Dick looks at me when he says "Good-night"? Or—no; that isn't the real point. The real one is, *Do* I care? Well, I guess I care. But you, Journal, are the only one who shall ever know it.

He has come back; it is two years since he was last in Milton. The last time he had a month's holiday, which left him three weeks here; the other week was spent in going and coming, for he was in Nebraska then. He says he feels like an Easterner now, for his work has taken him to Missouri (he builds trolly-car lines, like those in Boston, I believe, for the little cities out there); but Missouri hasn't seemed far enough East to let him come back oftener than when he first went West. When he first went I did not care so much, I suppose; at least I didn't reckon time greedily. How strange it seems now! but it is true: whole weeks went by in those days when I didn't think of him. Yet we were friends then too; quite as good friends as now. Only I felt differently about him, I suppose! Suppose? Oh, don't let us pretend to each other, you safe, safe pen and paper, and my heart! To some one, to some thing, I *must* speak! Somewhere I *will* be all myself! I love him! I love him! . . . . How dared I write that? It's a frightful word. But I'm glad. I wanted to look the dreadful thought in the eyes. I've seen it now; perhaps it will do me good. I'm not afraid to love him, though the word scares me. And, besides, no one knows.

October 6.—Yes, it is really true. No one knows. And how do you suppose I am sure of that ? Why, because every one—mother, and all the girls that I've helped to engage and marry and settle, even the one I've seen through her separation from her husband (that's Daisy)—all, all are poking me and pinching me and nagging me into *accepting* Dick ! Ah, I've played the part of old maid too well. These twelve years in which I've fought and scorned them, and swept my skirt clear of their odious ideas of marriage, have convinced them of too much. They have come to believe that because I don't look at the wrong ones, there never will be a right one. I have found the right one now, and he has not found me. I tell you the plain fact in that way, dear Journal. I don't mind adding that it's not in this way I tell it to my pillow. He came a fortnight ago to-night. When did I last sleep the night through ? It was on a Wednesday. He came on a Wednesday. Oh me ! how hot and wet one's pillow gets by two in the morning ! And there is still the long night. They wonder why I get up so early. It's not

86

because I'm rested. Oh, I'm tired, tired! How do other girls do who love men who don't love them? They don't. They don't allow themselves to. They have their pride. I've lost mine. And then they don't have a whole village at their heels, begging them to like the man just a little, entreating them to give him a chance. There, I've said it. Give him a chance! I blush even to write it. How can I?

October 10.—You see what I mean, you poor, patient Journal. I am being thrown at the head of the man I love (Oh, Dick, under my breath hear me say how I love you!) upon their wicked and revolting theory about marriage. I am to trade upon the weakness of men; I am to bring him to my feet; I am to allure, to call him on, to snare him—why not say it? I am to make love to him; I who love him, I who would die ten deaths rather than that he should know it. Oh, is it likely?

October 13.—Dick is just a little younger than I am, perhaps a year. We went to the village school together long ago. We were in the same class. He used to bring me apples; we ate them together straight on through the season, from the blossom to the Baldwin. And then there was the strawberry apple, which was good too, with its pretty streaks of red through the centre. Dick used to call them blushes, and to make comparisons. He doesn't make comparisons since he came back this time, and he is otherwise much changed. I like the changes. They only make him more utterly Dickily Dick. Well, Journal, you would like him too if you could see him.

What is he like? What is any young girl's dream like? What is the love of a youthful spinster like? Like the nicest thing there is. Dick is a man, you know. That's it. Except my father, he is the only quite man I know. There are male beings and men. He was a man even as a boy, when he fought Tommy Maeder for me, and charged a snowballing mob of boys in my defence, single-handed. I liked him then. He

knows that; he believes I still like him. I don't;
but he will never know the difference. Mamma
and Aunt Caroline and the girls have arranged
all that. Every time I meet him I say to myself:
" I will conquer this feeling—I will. I will be
natural with him. I will be myself." And every
time it is the same old story. I am not myself;
I am not any one at all. He doesn't recognise
me. I can see it. Why should he? I don't
recognise myself. I am like a person who longs
to shout, and can only produce dumb sounds.
All the natural outflow of my nature—there
really used to be one—seems dammed up the
moment we meet now. I am baffled. I almost
think I used to have a sort of charm for him
once; and if I ever had, it is there still
perhaps. But it might as well not be. It will
never reach him; the wires are down. It all
appears so strange that it somehow seems at
times as though it could not concern me. At
these times it seems another girl's story—the
story of a girl not less cruelly helpless—at which

I look on sadly. Ah, I've listened to other girls so long !

I shake mother ; but what good does that do? It's a feeling. You can't shake a feeling. It sounds like a simple thing to say to these eager, urgent, watchful girls, who come to see me every morning, and talk of nothing else. " It's not urging I need. What I need is his love, and you are making it impossible." But the only simple thing about it is its brevity. I could never say it, of course, and if I could they wouldn't understand. Didn't I engage them and marry them? Don't I know their impossible ideas about marriage ?—the ideas common among women, I mean? And my mother's ideas—yes, even my own dear mother's—are the same. In a way, I bear it better from her. As I said, her marriage has been a success. The results of the marriages of the others make advice from them an impertinence. I have learned that it isn't, though ; it is simply the married woman's view of marriage, which is one and the same the world over. They mean it for my good—they always make that plain— when they pluck at me in private and throw me at his head in public; and that they are killing me, instead, is just what I can't tell them.

They treat us as if we were engaged. I believe they come to the house when they know Dick is coming, in order to go away on his arrival and leave us *tête-à-tête.* They nod kindly to me as they make their adieus on these occasions, and include us both in a look of understanding. If we go out together—and on the whole it is less conscious, I have decided, to accept Dick's invitations than to refuse them —we are isolated at once by common consent, as if I weren't already cut off from him enough by my own feelings! Perhaps it is merely the unskilled rural way of doing a thing which might be carried off naturally enough in town; but it gives me the cold shivers. And do you think I can speak a natural word to Dick that evening? I don't know that I am more than common shy (though I'm not brazen either), but I have my woman's senses. I can't help that. And these things simply stupefy and paralyse all our intercourse.

In a village it is easy to bring the entire population to agreement upon questions of a certain kind. Since Dick's arrival my mother, my aunt, and the girls have unintentionally made it as plain to every one as if they had posted it at the town-hall, that they look upon Dick Lester as a man whom I might capture if I would. I put it grossly. They state it more prettily to me; but this is really what they mean. They are accustomed to add that it is my last chance—again putting it more politely.

Last night at the Unitarian fair I helped them out as " Rebecca at the Well," and from behind my curtain had the satisfaction of hearing young Mrs. McGregor (the wife of our doctor) say to Dick, " Isn't Miss Devius coming this evening?" I said that they treat us as if we were engaged. I should have said that they treat us as if we were married. And they think this the way to throw me into his arms! Of course he sees; an owl must see. Imagine our graceful, natural, and easy conversation! Ugh!

October 17.—I have just learned that Dick's vacation expires a week from to-day.

October 18.—Yes, of course he sees. My too amiable mother made up a party yesterday to go over to the lake. I declined to make one of the carriage company. But mother insisted. They put us together on the front seat, of course, and made Dick drive. I believe mother thinks Dick is the *driver* of his trolly cars. He does drive very well, because he does everything well, and on this occasion he gave his whole mind to it. I saw he had begun to feel my inexplicable conduct; but he said nothing then, and I could say nothing. I don't think we exchanged fifty words on the way to Lake Mesowree.

After luncheon on the shore—it's really a beautiful lake, hemmed in by the most gorgeous old hills—the company divided into rowing parties. You can imagine how they arranged it for Dick and me. He pulled for a mile or two in a silence which I made a number of efforts to break. But I could not force myself to speak. It has come to that. I can no longer so much as break a silence with this man whom I love, and whose reading of me I dread in every nerve. How he must wonder! But I am helpless. Stiff, formal, lifeless—that is what all our talk has become. It's a blight. I can do nothing with it. Two years ago, when he had been three years in the West, and came home on his first vacation, it was all so different. We met then on the sure footing of our childish friendship; there was the common liking to which we could both trust, and the common understanding. That is gone now, and we have nothing in its place. We have merely drifted into the doldrums.

If they had let us alone, I don't say that the other would have come ; but things have their natural way of blossoming, and love has come before of such relations. I suppose I must have loved him then—that is, before he went away. I was sure of it when he took my hand a little more than two weeks ago, the night he came back for this second time, and said in that deep, good, honest voice of his, "Well, Ellen ? " Ah, if they would but let me have him—if they would not snatch my love away, and cry it in the streets, so that every natural act becomes a shame to me, and I must seem to propose to him with every civil word I give him—well, everything might be different !

Oh, I say might ! I don't know. He might care ; he might not. But I could give him the chance my mother talks of in her awful ignorance of her daughter. I mean I could be myself; I could let things take their course. It is all that a woman has—that right : it does not seem a great privilege, does it ? But I am denied it.

95

This is the sort of thoughts that keep racing through my head when I am with Dick. I was watching him pull silently on with big sweeps of his strong arms, and I ought to have been chatting with him, like the sensible and lively person I really am, but I was thinking instead, and thinking thoughts which never helped any one to such conversation—thoughts which I hardly dared think in the same boat with him. It always seems to me that he must see through the thin partition between such thoughts and him, his eyes are so clear; and something he saw in my face seemed actually to make him speak after a moment. I remember very well that it was at that moment that I was making my eyes seem to see him far, far away again, and wondering how I should bear it. He was drifting, drifting steadily out of my reach in my fancy—it was the boat, I suppose, that gave me that idea—and I was standing on a beach stretching my helpless arms out to him, and crying after him to come back; and he was willing, or not unwilling, but he too was help-less. He was being quietly, and steadily, and pitilessly carried away from me. His question brought me back to an actual lake, and to a real Dick who was asking me ever so gently, in a kind way which is like no one's else, why I was so different lately. Of course I had known this must come some time; but between my sad vision and my surprise at the suddenness of the question, I was in a panic, and had to think how to make myself appear quite calm before I could answer his question.

I said the very idlest and stupidest thing I could have said, naturally.

"Am I changed?" I asked.

Then it lay with him to show me how I was changed; and he didn't lack circumstances for the accusation. It was impossible to answer him; I knew that from the start. But I really think it would have been easier if he hadn't been so generous through it all, so anxious not to wound me, and so solicitous for our old

G

friendship. He would hate to lose it, he said; he hoped I felt the same about it. O Dick! Dick!

For that one moment I wanted to be a man. In that one moment I would have given everything I possessed for the man's right to be honest.

I don't know what I said to him. I was thinking one thing and saying another, and what I said doesn't count except for its effect, which was to give him the impression that I was changed, and was conscious of it, and that there *was* a reason which I would rather not tell him. I can see now that that impulse in defence of modesty, which to women is like the instinct of self-preservation, forced me to let him believe that the change, if there was one, was perhaps the dumb protest of a decent woman against the intention he must perceive in those about me. I saw that, whatever I had intended he should believe—and I can never be sure now what it was—this was what he did finally arrive at. I saw it from the sympathy and the respectful understanding implied by his tone, his manner, everything. And as I sat there, watching him row on and on, I grew coldly, deadly sure that if there had ever been a chance for me to fight my way back to our old understanding—an understanding which now should include the new—it was gone. The half-truth he had got hold of was worse than any whole error. For half-truths there are no explanations.

Dick's glad, cordial manner—a complete change from the Dick of the drive over—was in itself a definite and kindly assurance that no explanations were needed. If he could have known how I longed to explain, and how miserably unexplained I remained after he had understood everything! That friendly effect of having understood everything was in all his bearing towards me until we parted that night in the cool darkness at my mother's door, and there he confirmed it in his lingering and

speaking hand-clasp. We drew near in spirit
at that moment, and again, as in the boat in the
afternoon, I seemed to see our destinies taking
form. But this time I saw clearly that we
might be all in all to each other, that he could
love me, that he *must* love me, if we could
know each other's hearts. But what his hand-
clasp was actually saying was that he understood — and everything ! Good heavens !
Everything !

October 21.—My mother has seen that we
have entered on a new phase. I think my be-
haviour, as she always calls it when it is a
question of men, had begun to discourage even
her ; not in itself, but through its obvious effect
on Dick. But since Dick has understood he is so
different, and we are so different together, in
appearance, that mother has taken heart. She
sees the kindness for me in all his bearing,
which now no one could help seeing ; what
she does not see is that she and the others
have made it impossible for me to assist at the

change of that kindness to anything nearer, in the way that all women assist at their love affairs by merely consenting to them. If I was incapable of a natural attitude with him before, what do you suppose I am now? If I could not let him love me before, has it been made easier for me? But mother, naturally, cannot see this, and I certainly cannot tell her. So she has been going over the whole matter with me this morning again, making a last despairing appeal. As if I could do for appeals what I can't do for my own heart.

Yet I pity mother. Even if she doesn't understand, I pity her. Ah! understand? You and I and our tears understand one another, don't we, Journal?

Dick comes daily now, and stays a long time, and is infinitely, tirelessly, agonisingly kind. Sometimes he is so kind that I feel as though I must scream. I really can't keep it up much longer. If he had not already set a day for going, I believe I should beg him to do me the

final kindness—the only one in his power—and
go at once! He would even do that for me.
He *does* like me; we talk of each other's lives;
we have such heart-searching talks about
everything but the only thing that matters; we
find each other's thoughts and feelings intui-
tively; we get along. Why shouldn't we? We
were made for each other, weren't we? That we
are not going to carry out the arrangement—
well, that's not our fault, is it? At least it's not
mine, and I'm sure it's not Dick's. I forgot to
say that I am quite, quite clear now that Dick
would have loved me. . . . .

October 24.—He came to see me last. He
wanted me to be his last impression of home,
he said. It was a chilly morning, such as comes
up here in the mountains towards the last of
October. The leaves on the hill we see from
our front windows have all fallen; they were
very gay three weeks ago—when he came. The
Seckel pears are just ripe. He wouldn't come
in; he held his hat in his hand as he came

into our hallway for a moment. In his other hand he carried a small hand-bag.

"So you're really going?" I said. He had said the night before that he would look in on his way to the station, and all the morning I had waited his coming, imagining just this scene. But, now that he was here, it was this that I found to say.

He looked into my eyes—Dick's honest, staunch look—and said, "Yes; it's been good to be at home."

"But it's good to be going back to work, too," I said. I did not find the courage for a look like his; my eyes halted at his chin.

"Of course; work is always good. But the best thing is old friends. These have been happy times, Ellen, seeing you again. I sha'n't soon forget our talks. I shall have time to remember them in Missouri."

"But you have the new friends there?" I wanted to hear him say it, and of course he said it, as he looked into my eyes and took my hand.

"They're not like the old," he said.

"No?" asked I.

"No. Good-bye." He took my hand in a wonderful, strong, warm, hearty grasp, and released it almost instantly.

"Good-bye," I said, following him to the door as he put on his hat.

"Good-bye."

At the gate he kissed his hand to me.

I.

BERNA was not allowed to see the papers until the tenth day. Then she read the story of his death in his own paper. Terror crept over her as she read, and she cast the *Telepheme* from her and buried her weak head in her hands, living over the anguish of that moment. She shuddered again with the hideous crash of the collision, and went whirling in his embrace down, down into a dizzy blackness, and then lay at the bottom of the Cañon, the wreck piled on top of them and round about them ; the air loud with the cowing noise of escaping steam, and wild with the shrieks of the dying. His poor white face stared up at her from under the wreckage yearning with love, horrid with pain, and his tortured lips framed the words which imposed a sacred duty on her future :

" Keep up the fight ! "

Aleck had left her everything he owned, they told her, and she knew why. It was not only as his promised wife, it was as the inheritor of his work; and a week later, when she was carried downstairs for the first time, she sent for Rignold, who had got out two issues of the *Telepheme* since the death of his chief, with no help but Barton's, and asked him to put her name at the head of the paper. For the next week's issue Rignold set up this legend to appear above the editorial notices :

" The Rustler Telepheme."

BY

BERNA MINTERMAN DEXTER.

FOUNDED BY ALEXANDER CHESTER.

Rignold turned his rules around the concluding line, making an oblong frame of black for it.

106

In making this explanation, we should not feel honest toward our readers in attempting to conceal a fact, no doubt already known to many of them, viz., the relation subsisting between the late and the present editor. It is due to all concerned that we should mention this, as it is because the present writer feels herself to be, in a true sense, the widow of the late editor, that she presumes to attempt the undertaking of carrying on a paper which, in his hands, has been such a power for good in this community.

This difficult post, assumed most reluctantly in response to a dying wish, we need not say is not taken up with any feeling of competence to the labours before us, nor with any feeling but that many others would fill the position more adequately and wisely. We are led to take hold of this work, where it was left off by Alexander Chester, solely out of respect for his memory, and with the belief that one who was privileged to know the hopes and plans for this town and this community which beat in that

great heart, may be able to carry them forward
—feebly indeed, but with a sympathy and understanding impossible to any stranger. The
present editor, in printing her name at the head
of this column, consecrates her life to the work
which fell a fortnight since from the palsied
hand of Alexander Chester. All Rustler knows
what that work was. The entire future of the
town is bound up in it. We must have the
railroad. The Three C's must come our way.
Into this cause Alexander Chester poured his
life-energy ; to it he gave all he was, or hoped
to be. As the officer on the field of battle
snatches up the weapon that has fallen from his
dead captain, and presses on, so we take up
this work, with malice toward none, and with
charity for all ; but presenting a solid front to
the common enemy, resolved that Topaz shall
not be allowed to accrete to herself this new
source of wealth and strength. It is a life and
death struggle : we know it, and Topaz knows
it. United and unanimous as we are, we have

only to continue to assert our rights and to make the advantages of Rustler duly known, to secure the Colorado and California Central without a doubt.

In conclusion, the writer wishes to thank personally all the late editor's fellow-townsmen for the generous tribute of sorrow and regret at his death manifested by one and all. She accepts it not merely as a tribute to a noble man, but to the purpose which he had most nearly at heart. The value and importance of that purpose to Rustler could not be more clearly shown than by these unsolicited tributes. They warm the heart of his successor in this editorial chair, and strengthen us for the work before us. That it may be worthy, in however humble a degree, of the man who has gone from us, and of the town of Rustler, is the hope of

BERNA MINTERMAN DEXTER.

The "copy" from which this was to be set up had reached Rignold stained with the tears it had cost her. He read it through with a queer feeling in his throat, then closed and locked the office (Barton, the foreman, and the boy had gone for the night), and lighting the lamp over his case, set it himself. The careful, girlish manuscript, traced among the tell-tale blurs, on little sheets of pink note-paper, impressed at the top with a twisted " B. M. D." in gold, was not a sight for other eyes than his.

The sense of what was and what was not good newspaper work had rubbed off on Rignold in eight years' service as one of the compositors, and five years as the foreman, of a New York evening paper. The weekly he had come West to establish had failed ; but that was because he had chosen the wrong town. Drifting back eastward by way of Colorado, he had been content to accept Chester's offer, and on another man's paper had displayed the qualities which, if the mines of his Idaho town had panned out richer, would have made his own journal successful. Chester and he had become friends, and had remained so, though it was Chester who finally won Berna ; and it was not the smallest testimony to the love that dared warm to life again with the tragic death of his friend, that, denying himself the habit of thought bred by his newspaper experience, Rignold now set Berna's article without an attempt to edit it, and without so much as a preliminary mechanical motion toward the waste-basket. To know so well what his old managing editor would have done with the poor girl's editorial did not make it less pathetic. The thought caused her rather to seem more helpless and more dependent on him, and gave him reason to notify to himself in plain terms that the *Telepheme* was to be made a success under its new editor, if it cost a leg. As his sensitive printer's hand, with its five eyes, wove back and forth over the case, he smiled fondly to himself at the little literary graces of her writing, as he often did at the little literary frills of her talk. They were so

112

much part of all his knowledge and thought of
her that he could not have dissociated them
from her without doing violence to the sanctuary
in which he kept his love. Her faults were as
dear to him as her virtues—dearer perhaps,
because more accessible than the lofty qualities
for which he adored her. He couldn't smile
affectionately upon her virtues ; her faults
seemed warm and near.

Nevertheless, he declared to himself, as he
stooped beneath the lamp that gathered its
rays under the scorched green shade to throw
them on Berna's pages, that he was a fool—a
chartered, twice-dyed and double-branded
idiot—to allow himself to have any business
dealings with a woman. Looking out through
the window of the Disbrow Block, from which
the *Telepheme* regarded the town whose life it
recorded, he wondered how they would take it
—the people of Rustler, going in and out, and
to and fro, below there. The town, engaged
under an electric noonday in the feverish play

which, in mining camps, is so much more active
to the outward eye than the day's business,
would make up its mind precious quick; Rignold only wondered which way. Would their
sympathy for her situation, their liking for the
grit with which she faced it, their reverence for
womanhood, carry her through? Would these
excellent sentiments weigh against more vital
considerations when it came to the scratch?
Would they finally feel that they could afford
them? The *Telepheme* was of course the
fighting organ through which the railroad was
to be brought to Rustler, if it was brought at
all. Would they trust the fight to a woman?
Rignold sighed his heavy doubt to the dumb
types in their boxes, and went on setting
Berna's exotic editorial, with its singular mix-
ture of easily-come-by newspaperese and far-
brought literosity, and its still stranger mingling
of shrewd reasoning and high-flown inconclu-
siveness.

When he had pulled the first copy of that

week's paper on the old Washington hand-press which Chester had originally brought from the East with him, he sent it down to Berna, who lived alone with her mother near the end of the main street of Rustler. The house was an un-clapboarded two-storey frame structure, painted a reddish brown, not unlike the colour of the rocks jutting from the mountain that hung above the roof. If you think of a giant pair of pincers standing upright and wide open, you will know how Rustler lay; Big Chief sprang into the air on one side, Ticknor's Mountain on the other: between was a narrow crotch, and deep down in it cuddled the town. The greater part of the inhabitants lived on Berna's street; but the miners' cabins, built beside the shafts of a hundred mines, carried a steadily rising overflow up the flanks of the two moun-tains. The house in which Berna lived was set close to the street, six feet from the board side-walk that ran in front of her pink palings. Within this narrow space she had tried, before

Aleck's death, to make a bed of pansies grow with the help of water from the irrigating ditch that raced by the house on its way to the main ditch, supplying Topaz with its water; but the flowers had withered since the accident. As she lay on the sofa in her parlour, torn alternately by her grief for Aleck and by her own pain, she heard, after each shift at the mines, the clumping noise of miners' boots go by on their way to or from the Elegant Booze, the Honeycomb, and Uncle Dick's—establishments where one got two glasses of beer for a quarter and a good deal of faro for a ten-dollar bill.

The injury which she had sustained in the railway accident left her good hours, but oftener put her to the torture; and when her mother handed her her first issue, she was unable to do more for the first hour than gaze steadfastly at the heading. The sight of the familiar title made the thought of Aleck overwhelmingly poignant; tears welled into her eyes as she stared at the folded white sheet lying outside the blue Navajo blanket that covered her, and she turned at last from the sight in misery.

She was nevertheless helpless against the literary pleasure that tingled through her when she finally took courage to read over her editorial, though she was ashamed of it. It was not for the excitement and interest of writing that she had determined to keep the *Telepheme* alive, and to shape it into a force which should carry on Aleck's work, as a son carries on the work of his father. It was as Aleck's child that she was to watch over it. She reproached herself, but finally forgave herself, with the thought that it was through his own pleasure in his work that Aleck had succeeded, and that she must find a like joy in it, if she was to be in any sort worthy to follow in his steps. She did not need to stimulate a happiness in writing; she liked it; until she had become engaged to Aleck it had been her ambition to be a "magazinist." Berna was ne of the half-turned-out women

117

who begin to be common in the West. Her
mind had been educated ; but her intelligence,
her taste, her perceptions, remained to all in-
tents as undeveloped as a Kaffir's. She was
charming ; but if she had been as cultured as
she supposed herself, it would have been impossible to associate with her. Her charm lay in
her simple-mindedness, in her unselfishness and
kindness and devotedness and pluck ; but what
she really liked in herself was her complicated-
ness. Some of this she had endeavoured to explain through the Iowa magazine which printed
her earliest contributions to the press, just after
she had "been graduated," as she called it, from
Miss Drewett's New England seminary. The
contributors to this magazine were almost
all women, and were, without exception, complicated.

Her mother came in as she laid down the
paper to ask if she would see Ben. Berna drew
her shawl about her, and nodded, brightening
with pleasure. The room in which she lay was

stiffly furnished in a stamped red plush, but a comfortable old sofa, covered with chintz, had been moved in for her out of the dining-room. On the walls were two cheap paintings of the Yosemite, Berna's graduating diploma under glass, and a photograph (framed in a deep black walnut moulding) of her father in the uniform of a lieutenant of volunteers : the artist had picked out the epaulettes in gold and touched the cheeks with carmine.

Mrs. Dexter asked if she didn't think it would fret her to see Ben.

"You know the doctor said——"

"Yes ; I know, mother. But if I am to carry on this work I mustn't mind the doctor. Perhaps it will kill me ; but if it does, it must. I shall only give in my report to Aleck a little sooner."

The tears, against which she had not yet learned to school herself, once more stood in her eyes.

"Gracious, child ! I don't believe Aleck ever in this world expected you to go on with the

Telepheme. How could he think a woman could do such a thing?"

"I don't know, mother. But he trusted me to do it, and I can't be false to him."

"Well, you'll kill yourself," she repeated, weakly. "Why can't you let Ben do it? He's willing and able."

"How can you suggest such a thing, mother? You know he's a stranger in the town."

"I don't care if he is. He knows printing."

"Of course. But he can't *feel* as we Rustler-ites do, mother. You know that. The railroad is nothing to him."

"No; I suppose not," she owned, downcast. But in a moment she added, with more spirit, "There's lots of folks in the town that it's plenty to, though. Some of 'em would be glad to edit the paper if you'd let 'em."

"They wouldn't know how."

"Well, do you know how?"

"No," answered Berna, shaking her hair loose from her face, raising her head, and drawing in

a deep inspiration; "*but I've heard Aleck
talk !*"

"Oh dear !" exclaimed Mrs. Dexter, rising
with the feebleness of rheumatic limbs, wearied
with a life's hard work, "I suppose we've got to
bear it. But I do hope you'll be careful of yourself, and not overdo. I wish I wasn't so afraid
you'd lose the little money your father left us in
the 'Sons of Honour,'" she added, pathetically.

"But I sha'n't, mother. I've explained that
so often. I shall only use Aleck's money. He
left me enough to keep up the paper with.
When I've sold the 'Lady Berna' mine I shall
have plenty."

"I know you say that, Berna, and you think
you mean it. But when once you get started
you can't tell what you'll do. Look at Aleck !
I'm sure he would have pawned the coat off his
back any minute for the sake of his paper ; and
I don't believe you'll do any less for *his* sake
when the time comes."

"Yes, mother," said Berna, soothingly, laying

a hand in her mother's work-roughened palm. "Show Ben in ; won't you, please ?"

Rignold appeared at the door in a moment, halting on the threshold with his slouch hat in his hand.

"Come in, Ben !" Her voice was still feeble. Mrs. Dexter pushed him gently in from behind. "I'm so glad to see you," Berna continued, putting forth her wasted hand from under the shawl. "Be seated, won't you ?"

But Rignold did not immediately seat himself. He stood looking down into her face with a tender studiousness. The high colour, which in health shone brilliantly against the creamy pallor and childlike smoothness of skin that often goes with auburn hair and blue eyes, had gone in her illness; her usual roundness of figure and plumpness of cheek were gone also. What remained was the bright vitality of her deep blue eyes, and the extraordinary beauty of her abundant hair, which she was wearing coiled in thick, burnished masses of reddish-brown or brownish-red, as one chose, or as the light served.

The man standing above her was tall and spare, with a fine figure, a little stoop-shouldered from bending at the case, but erect when he stood. He carried his large round head well back; his dark hair curled a little in receding from a high, clear brow; his brown eyes encountered the observer with a singularly honest, straightforward look. He shook hands as if he meant it.

" I didn't feel as if I ought to come. But I didn't see my way to not coming," he said.

" I see I must tell you one thing right away, Ben. You're not to think of me as a woman." A distressed whimsical smile appeared on his face, which she answered with, " I mean, I'm an editor like anybody else. There are plenty wiser and more adequate, as I said in my editorial. I shall be incompetent in a good many ways at first, and I'm sure to do foolish things. But there are men in the profession who began with less knowledge than I have now, and who have succeeded ; and there are others who began with more knowledge, and have failed. I ask no favours that were not accorded to them. I only wish to be judged fundamentally on the same basis."

" I don't feel any call to judge you, Berna," answered Rignold, with a smile, as he took a chair. " But if I did, I don't see but I'd have to judge you as a woman. It's all right to say 'think of you as a man.' But you ain't a man, and that's just what I like about you, and what makes me want to help you, if I can. You are a woman, but you've got a man's sand."

" Don't say that, Ben. I haven't got Aleck's."

" See here ! Do you think Aleck, or any other man, for the matter of that, would have taken up a job like this two weeks after he'd lost the only thing that made life worth while to him, and taken it up without turning a hair and without ruffling a feather to call attention to it ? If you do, you size men up for a better breed than they are."

A groan burst from her, and she covered her face quickly with her hands.

" I am a fool to talk like that ! " he cried.

" No, no ! It does me good. You under-stand. Every one won't, perhaps. They won't think it decent—the ladies particularly. They will say I don't mourn truly for Aleck ; as if this weren't the best and only mourning for him ! As if it weren't just because I care so much that I can't justify myself in wasting *his* time in tears ! That's the way I feel, Ben—that husband and wife have a double time in this world ; and be-cause both times belong to them and to God while they both live, it's the happiness and the sacred responsibility of the survivor to answer for both times when one time is—is frus-trated."

Rignold, resolved as he was to keep his wish to help her disinterested and separate from his love for her, could not help wincing at this,

while he smiled at her words. He saw, as if
looking into the future through a rift in the
curtain, how they would be constantly running
up against this spectral third presence in their
intercourse, and how he should be "stumped"
by it—perhaps for always. It was a presence
that he had loved in life; but the presence of
the man she had preferred to him, while it was
still open to her to choose, and the presence of
the man who he must believe was to be per-
manently dear to her. He wanted to cry out
against this folly of devotion; he wanted to say
how crazy it seemed to him—this duty to the
dead, this conscience about a ghost. Perhaps
he might have said it, if he hadn't guessed in
time that what he took for moral indignation
was probably a good deal more like simple
jealousy. With his accustomed squareness, he
said to himself that if he had gone the way of
Aleck he should have hungered for just such
devotion in his place. Perhaps it wouldn't last
for ever, and if it did, it was still good to look

126

forward to the prospect of working by her side, helping her where he could.

He spoke the sympathetic words that came to him in answer to her declaration ; and then he said : " I suppose you've figured out how you're going to work this thing—lying down ? "

II.

BERNA'S first issue was published on the following morning, and by afternoon fifteen new subscribers had handed in their names at the office of the *Telepheme.* One or two enthusiasts even paid up long overdue subscriptions, and ordered the paper sent them for the following year ; and Mrs. Dexter was kept busy informing the ladies who called on Berna that as yet she could see nobody. The town was in a state of emotional sympathy which it would gladly have expended in taking the horses from Berna's carriage, and dragging it through the streets, if the plucky young editor had owned the carriage or the horses.

Rustler still trembled with the memory of the accident; it had scarcely buried its dead, and the desolation of the bereaved families echoed in its one mountain street. Chester had enjoyed with the inhabitants the repute of a vigorous personality, offering its strength unreckoningly to the town's ambition; and Berna, who had been less popular hitherto in the town on her own account, had, before the publication of her first issue, gained, through the circumstances surrounding her lover's death in her presence on the day before their wedding-day, an honour beyond anything that Chester had known. It was only necessary that she should rise from her bed of pain, and, in the midst of her grief, take up Aleck's work, to constitute her a heroine. Rignold had been sure that they would like her " sand," but he had not reckoned sufficiently, he found, with their pleasure in piecing a romance out of any event which concerns a woman

128

publicly. Her devotion to Aleck's memory,
which to the women of the place seemed (against
Berna's expectation) "just splendid," won the
profane praise of the men at the Elegant Booze
and on the street corners, not merely as showing
the right stuff, but as showing it on behalf of the
town. They rolled her name relishingly on their
tongues in their perception of this final right-
ness; like the Greeks, it warmed their loyal
pride to know that even their women were
patriotic. They saw Berna looking well in a
newspaper article on Rustler; and this created
her part of the town's "material," part of its
capital for booming purposes.

Berna was made very happy by her success,
and slept that night the sleep of those widowed
queens who have had to doubt for the first
tremulous hour of sovereignty the allegiance of
subjects that mourn a king. Aleck's path lay
freely before her; she had only to tread it
worthily. The town where she had first known
Aleck and where they had made a grave for him,

the town which he had loved and served, the
town for which he had been ready to shed
his blood and for which she was now so willing
to shed hers, the town that he had left to her
care—the town had accepted her.   But she put
aside merely agreeable thoughts, and day-dreams
of what she would yet do for Rustler, with the
morning, and settled down soberly to her work.
It was very well for every one to wish her luck,
but Berna had a hard-headed little theory that
she must make her own luck, and she went about
the preparation of a rousing railroad editorial in
Aleck's old manner.

The system on which the paper was to be
conducted had been fixed upon between her and
Rignold at their conference. Its policy was, of
course, to be guided wholly by her ; she was to
take complete charge ; all the leading editorials
were to be hers, and she was to supervise the
news columns. Rignold was to look after
the "locals," write the minor editorials, find
advertisements, superintend the job printing and

manage the business department, and in general
represent her to Rustler. Berna had certainly
cut out a large undertaking for herself; but in
her ignorance she had let Rignold load upon his
willng shoulders an heroic proportion of the work.
He could not tell her how glad he would have
been to double his stint for her sake ; but he
could go forth to scour the town for emotional
advertising ; and (not to let Berna's boom pass
without immediate practical result) he did this
on the morning her first number was published.
Sensible of the vicissitudes to which such
enthusiasms as Rustler's for Berna are liable,
he declined to accept any advertisement, under
present conditions, for a shorter period than one
year ; if they wanted a newspaper they must
expect to pay for it, he said ; and if they really
believed in the town, and had the courage of
their convictions, they would probably pay for
it in advance. His theory did not meet with
universal acceptance, but it met with nearly six
columns' worth of acceptance, and this, as he

explained in the next issue under the heading of " Our Boom," struck him as handsome. He let slip, in the course of this brief editorial, enough restrained self-gratulation on behalf of the *Telepheme*, and enough general good feeling and modest sense that Topaz would never have toed the mark so squarely in a similar emergency, to have filled one side of the paper, diluted as an inferior man would have diluted it. Rignold wrote carefully, with the feeling constantly upon him that he was working for larger issues than the success of Rustler or the *Telepheme*. He found Berna in the point of his pencil when he would muse on his next sentence, and the white paper was covered with her name before he wrote a line upon it.

He had not needed to inquire his fate in the time before Berna's engagement to Aleck ; and he withheld himself now with a sensitive scrupulousness from so much as the semblance of love-making. He felt in the weeks that followed that he must not allow himself to think directly

of her yet ; but the habit of thinking of her in-
directly lapsed at times into the most straightway
regard of her. At these seasons, however, her
own attitude corrected his unconsciously; for
the profound preoccupation of her whole being
with Aleck's memory must have baffled the
warmest lover. Rignold's love for her, in fact,
made him feel almost foolish in her presence,
as if he were trying to catch the attention of an
oblivious animal or child. Her detachment
from the ordinary affairs of the world sometimes
frightened him ; she was eating her heart out
for her lost lover, and the only sign of it that
she allowed any one to see was her joy in events
which would have given him joy. It was, of
course, chiefly in connection with the *Telepheme*
that Rignold witnessed the daily expressions of
her simple faithfulness to his dead friend ; and
it was in work for the *Telepheme*—that is, in
work for her—that he tried to forget her devotion to the spirit of another man, or tried to
wish that she might never lose it. He could

like it, as he liked everything about her, though it made him miserable and impatient.

It was perhaps his good fortune that, though Berna made it difficult for him to manage himself, this soon became, on the whole, rather simpler than to manage her paper. His young editor's word was "development," and it was pathetic to him to see how she pursued this idea of Aleck's, as she did other ideas derived from the same source, without the strength or the balancing sense and shrewdness which had enabled Aleck to give such words actuality. She became, as the months went by, and as she gained a measure of wisdom from her mistakes and successes, by no means a hopelessly bad newspaper man (as she liked to call herself). She had enterprise and assiduity, and the wish to print the news ; and her still stronger wish to make her "diction elegant" she did not allow to interfere seriously with these good qualities. Her real trouble, from a financial point of view, was that she wished to print more news than

the paper could afford, or than Rustler could
pay for. Having imbibed from Aleck his
belief that the best was none too good for
Rustler, she endeavoured to give the *Telepheme*
the catholic tone of the weekly edition of a New
York daily. Refusing Rignold's earnest suggestion, that they rely upon a patent outside, or
at worst upon plate matter, for the better part
of their miscellany, she spent the long hours on
her sofa, scissors in hand, culling interesting
items of news, and what she had learned from
Rignold to call " good stories," from her exchanges—guided in her selection, it is to be
feared, by the taste of Miss Drewett's rather
than by a vision of what Rustler would probably
like to read. Scandals, hangings, prize fights,
murders, and all other items of a too vivid
interest she excluded ; and the *Telepheme*
became that ensample of purity and social
health for which we all pretend we are longing.
One whose reading was confined to Berna's
paper might conveniently have imagined him-

self resident in a good and harmless world, in which was no evil, save that engendered by Topaz. She tried to atone for this, which Rignold taught her to regard, from the counting-house standpoint, as the deadly sin, by engaging a weekly telegraphic letter from Denver. It was sent on the morning the paper went to press, and contained all the latest news.

About this they had many discussions, wherein she met Rignold's objections with arguments in which Aleck's slangy wisdom often mingled curiously with her graduating essay view of life, and her knotted pink-ribbon manner of expression. His suggestion that the Denver letter constituted an expense not justifiable by a circulation three times their own, and (as it didn't bring them a subscriber) that it involved a loss rather larger than the other loss it was designed to set right, she met with something like impatience.

" Do you mean to advise me," she asked, "to do the little thing rather than the great one?

Do you really wish me to run a paper on anything but large ideas? Do you expect me to
give our readers only what they already want
and have learned to expect? The man who
attempts to be merely up to the day in the
West is going to get left; he must be up to
to-morrow ! "

As the town looked on at these developments
in the *Telepheme*, its first sentiment of enthusiasm began to take a very faint chill of
bewilderment. The catholic tone by which
Berna set such store was indifferent to its
citizens, and they could have got along with less
diction if they could have been furnished with
more sensation. They fortunately continued,
however, to admire and rejoice in her railroad
editorials. Heaven knows how she wrote them !
Her own theory was that she didn't; she
ascribed their authorship reverently to the inspiration of Aleck. It was true, at all events,
that he never seemed so near to her as when
she was penning them; and if for no other

reason than this, the conduct of the *Telepheme* would have given her great happiness. Her glib denunciations of Topaz, her ready magnifications of Rustler, her solid reasoning about the advantages which the Three C's would enjoy if it should finally come where the *Telepheme* was edited, had a man's cogency and fire ; the thin substance of her cleverness seemed penetrated as she wrote on the theme of the railroad by a kind of trance horse-sense. On the streets of Rustler these editorials were sometimes called "corkers," and sometimes "howlers"; but this did not represent a divided mind. They were, in a way, more effective than any similar work by a man would have been, for no man could have been so impudent or so ferocious. The seal of their success was at length set upon them when the other papers of the State began copying them. Berna of course copied back thier praise into the *Telepheme*, and the town simply licked its chops. To have given the quarrel between

Rustler and Topaz the dignity of a State fight, at which the whole population of Colorado might be fancied to be looking on, was a service for which it was felt **Berna** deserved well (if everybody could know the real merits of the case, no one could doubt which way the railroad would go) ; and she began at once to retrieve some of her lost popularity.

When, therefore, beginning at the end of a few months to sit up a little every day, though still not strong enough to go out, she broached the plan of re-organising her old " Culture Club,'" she met with such a response from the ladies as she had not dared expect.

The club had gained but a mild success before the illness of its founder ; the subjects were felt by the ladies to be rather stiff ; but even the new members now took kindly to the young editor's proposal of papers on " The Heroines of George Eliot," and " England's Early Mythic History," and to a suggested conversation, .to be led by Berna, ⟨n " The

Relation of Men and Women in Homer."
Perhaps, however, Berna's announcement of a
kind of learned game to be played at their
meetings in off-weeks, in the evenings, when
the men came late for oysters, proved more
distinctly popular. Rignold, observing these
things, and looking on the success of the club
as a sign, began to hope that, in spite of a
mad system of expenditure, the paper might
pull through without borrowing capital beyond
the $2000 obtained from the sale of the " Lady
Berna."

These were happy days of prosperity and
power and influence for Berna ; the circulation
of the *Telepheme* increased, and the town itself
began to grow again after a long season of depression. Berna allowed herself to ascribe both
growths in part to her own exertions, and looked
on the new-comers (for Aleck) with a double air
of proprietorship, as *Telepheme* population and
as *Telepheme* subscribers. She instituted a
quiet monthly census of her own, publishing the

results when favourable, and this became one of the most popular features of the paper in Rustler, being the better liked when it began to excite the uneasy derision of Topaz. The truth was, that the mines of Ticknor's Mountain and Big Chief, always fairly well to do, were now making large shipments of high-grade ore, and as the *Telepheme* never concealed anything of this sort, a certain tendency of the floating population of surrounding towns toward Rustler began to be observable.

Rignold, though he could not share his editor's confidence in the continuance of these good times for the town and the paper, made them as good as he knew how for himself by seeing a great deal of Berna. He helped and served her about the paper with untiring energy and a simple patience, and she recognised his goodness with gratitude ; but he knew that she conceived of it all as done for Aleck, in the same way that she did it all for Aleck, and he knew that she was grateful on Aleck's behalf. The

situation offered so little satisfaction to him that
he found it hard to be sorry in the first moments,
when the change came. But in fact he was
sorry, and if not for the change, then for her.

The current, which had turned in her favour,
gave signs for a month of turning the other way
before it finally did turn ; but when the change
came it fell upon her with the suddenness of a
thing unexpected and unimagined. The first
word of it reached her one evening as she sat
by her lamp thinking out the editorial for the
next week's issue, while she rocked to and fro
in her spacious rocker, walled in by her mother
with pillows, and ran through her State exchanges.

" It is rumoured that Rustler is to have a new
paper. They are getting tired, it seems, of having the town represented by a woman."

Her eye fell upon this item in one of the
papers which two months before had copied ex-
tracts from her railroad editorials with approval.

142

Rignold, looking in a quarter of an hour later for his customary weekly chat with her about the contents of the next issue, found her still staring dumbly at the newspaper. She looked up at him with blind eyes. Then in a moment she asked :

" Did you know about this ? "

" What ? " pretended Rignold.

She tapped the paper decisively with her forefinger without speaking, while she gazed at him in silence.

" Yes."

" Why didn't you tell me ? "

" I didn't see what good it could do."

" You would have told Aleck ? "

" That's so."

" Then why not me ? "

" Why, it's altogether different, Berna."

" Different ? Sit down. How different ? "

" Every way. I didn't want to hurt your feelings."

" You mean I was a woman. That's true.

143

But I haven't any less at stake on that account. I've more—twice as much. You forget Aleck."

" I'm not likely to do that," retorted Rignold, stung.

" What do you mean?"

" Good Heaven, Berna! Don't take it like this!"

"You mean I should remind you of him if you forgot. I suppose you're right. I should. I do talk of Aleck. I'm editing his paper; I'm trying humbly to live out his life for him. How can I help it? I can't forget him if the town does."

" Pshaw, Berna! The town ain't forgetting him. But it has to think of itself, or it thinks it has."

"And so they try to kill his paper?"

Rignold dropped his eyes. " I suppose they don't think it's his paper."

Berna started in her seat. " Have I put myself forward too much? Have I made too much of myself and too little of him? Yes; I was afraid of that."

" No, no! Lord knows you've made enough of Aleck. You've put him first everywhere. The town just don't want a woman for an editor. There's the whole of it, Berna, without trimmings. I know it's hard on you—awful hard, after all you've done and spent and suffered to give 'em a good paper, and to keep up Aleck's name, and boom the town and bring the railroad. But towns ain't grateful ; you know that as well as I do ; and I don't suppose Rustler's any exception. Look here ! this is the way it is. They want the Three C's, don't they? Well, they think they stand a better show to get it if they have another sort of paper and have a man to edit it. They think it'll look better outside. I suppose it will. But they won't get a paper the equal of the *Telepheme* in a hurry—not if they put two men on to edit it."

" Oh, what do I care how much better or worse it is? They won't let me do Aleck's work."

"They can't stop it."

"They don't want it. It's the same thing. I've offered the town my life ; I've offered them all my love and all my service ; and they"—her lip trembled—"they don't want it. It's not for myself I'm hurt ; it's the rejection of Aleck through me. They don't want *him* either. He's done all he could for them, and they're done with him. He brought them to a place where they could get along without him ; and now I've brought them a little farther, and they can do without me. Oh, Ben !"

She gave a little gasp and gulph, and suddenly buried her face.

Rignold leapt forward from his chair and laid a hand on hers. "Drop it, Berna ! Give it up and let them go their own ungrateful way. You're wasting your life on them, and what could they ever give you in return, if they did their best ?"

"Give me ! Do you suppose I want anything ?" She looked up fiercely through her

146

tears. "I've got to get my living and Ma's out of the paper, and that I'll take, for the laboure is worthy of his hire. But that's all. Aleck worked for the love of it; he fought for the town the same way a soldier fights for the flag. He wasn't thinking of rewards. 'It ain't boodle I'm after.' He always used to say it, and it was true. And after that, do you think I could—could"—(she caught her breath and stifled a sob, as her rhetoric returned to her with her self-command)—"could palter with the question of recompense? I don't want to be paid, Ben. I want to be let do it."

"Well, no one can prevent you. It's a free country. You can go on publishing the *Telepheme* just the same, if they do issue another paper alongside of it. Plenty of towns have two papers that can't rightly support one."

"I know it, Ben—I know it! Foolish towns, wicked towns—towns that have no respect for themselves or their cause! They divide their forces in the face of the enemy, and fight each

147

other when they ought to be fighting the common foe. That shall never be said of Rustler. It was the *town* that Aleck loved ; it wasn't his paper, and it wasn't himself. And I should be unworthy of him if I couldn't be glad to bury my pride in the paper, and all the ties that bind me to it through Aleck, and kill the *Telepheme* to-morrow, if it can help the town. If I can serve Rustler better by lying down and letting it trample on me, than by standing up and fighting for her, that's my place. I only want to be sure."

" Don't you be sure of it, Berna ! Don't you think it ! It ain't true. But; all the same, I'd give it up. The town *can't* support two papers, that's a fact ; and if it don't, and if it's the *Telepheme* that goes to the wall, you will have spent all the money that Aleck left, and perhaps your mother's insurance money too, before you're done, and have nothing left to live on I don't want to see you come to that, Berna ; and, if you're willing for yourself, you won't be for your mother, if you think a minute."

" Stop ! stop ! I'm not going to spend Ma's money. When I've spent Aleck's I'll give it up. But what you say puts my duty before me. I *must* spend Aleck's ! I mustn't, I daren't take the town's word for it that they're tired of Aleck and of me, until I've spent all that's left in giving them a chance to take that back—for Aleck's sake ! " she added devoutly. " They've changed once ; they may change again. Who knows ? What was it that made them change this time, Ben ? " she inquired, as if coming to the question of Rustler's altered temper for the first time.

" Oh, silliness ! You don't want to know.

" Ben ! " she cried, incriminatingly, " stop sparing me ! Tell me."

" Topaz kept joking them on their lady editor. You must have seen the *Telegram.*"

" Of course. But what then ? "

" Why, the other papers took it up. A weekly

paper's got to have copy. You know that, Berna."

"Certainly; I've seen all that, as it came along in the State exchanges from week to week. But I never thought the town would be cowardly enough to mind it. Oh, shame on them!"

"No; that ain't fair, Berna. It seems foolish; but it wasn't for themselves, really. You can see that, if you stop and think. They were afraid of its effect on the railroad. A town that wants a railroad can't afford to be made fun of by the press of the whole State. A railroad's a serious business; you've got to be worthy of it all round."

"Of course. But my railroad editorials aren't a bit poorer than when the whole press of the State quoted and praised them, and Rustler went wild with delight over them. Nothing has changed." She paused thoughtfully. "But I don't want Rustler to be made fun of—not on my account, nor anybody's. It *will* hurt the town. I must stop that. But they might have trusted me to! Why didn't they come to me squarely, and tell me that I was injuring the place? They might have believed that there are some things I care more for than myself; they might have known I'd have remedied the trouble, or stepped down and out. Do you mean to say, Ben, that they have the courage to give this as their reason? Why, they'll hurt the town more that way than any way. They'll be the laughing-stock of every paper in Colorado, from that one-page little rag they're getting out in the new camp on Eagle River—what's it's name?—Flux, to the *Rocky Mountain News.*"

" No," said Ben, dropping his eyes into the soft hat he twirled round and round in his fingers, " they don't *say* that's their reason ?"

" What do they say ? "

" If you'll excuse me, Berna, I guess I won't go into that."

" But I can't excuse you.

"Oh, well——" began Rignold, desperately, and stopped.

"Why, what's the matter, Ben?" she asked in bewilderment, watching the uneasy flush mount to his forehead. "Is it something personal? Is it something disgraceful?"

"Good heavens, no! It ain't disgraceful. But it ain't a thing for me to tell you, unless I tell you something else at the same time."

"Tell me both things."

Ben shook his head. "You wouldn't like it."

"Try me," said Berna, persuasively.

The breath was coming fast in Rignold's throat. He made two beginnings, and paused helplessly. "It wouldn't do any good," he said at last.

"Why, Ben, I never saw you behave like this. What's the matter?"

"Oh, love's the matter, Berna—love for you, that's killing me. You don't want it. You've got no more use for it than Rustler has for the *Telepheme*. I tell you because you ask me;

but I know well enough there ain't room for another paper in *your* town. I know the field belongs to Aleck. It's right; I ain't got nothing to say against it." He lowered his eyes again.

"Ben!" gasped Berna. Then in a moment she added another name.

"Of course! Of course! I know it, I tell you! I was a fool to say anything. But you would have it. The town says it ain't right that we should be so much together, and work the paper alongside each other, and not be married. They don't think I'm in love with you. They never guess that. And they know what you feel about Aleck, anyway. All they say is, it ain't proper. I couldn't tell you the one, you see, without telling you the other. I've told you both now, and I guess I might as well go."

He rose to his feet, but Berna stopped him. "Wait, Ben!" She laid on his coat sleeve the hand which would have detained him at the gate of heaven. "Good Ben! Sit down again—

won't you?—and we'll talk of this. It's awful—coming so suddenly. Give me a moment." He dropped back into his seat with reluctance.

She locked her hands distressfully in her lap. "But I don't see how we're going to talk of it! Oh, *Aleck!*"

"Sure! It ain't treating him right even to discuss it. I was his friend, and you were the same as his wife. I know that's the way you feel; and partly that's the way I feel myself. And so it ain't decent—what I tell you—but it's the truth. I love you, Berna, and I have loved you ever since long before Aleck and you were engaged. I held my tongue then, and I gave you up to him in my own mind, and if he'd lived you'd never have known what your marriage cost one man. But he didn't live. I wish he had. I can say that truly. I never wished his death; and when he was brought home to us here, that awful day, I took a hurt I haven't got over yet. But he is dead, Berna; and I'm alive, and if I'm to go on living, I can no more do it

154

without loving you, than I could go on living with my heart wanting in my side."

"Oh, Ben, I'm very sorry. You've been so good to me—so good! I've always thought it was for Aleck. But if it was for me, and you were saying No to this feeling all the time, and keeping it back for his sake, then I honour you for it, and—and I thank you. But what are we going to do, Ben?"

Rignold could not keep back a smile at this question of a child. "Oh, girlie! if you leave it to me——"

She gave him a long, absent look. "Yes, I know," she said at last. "Of course, I can't leave it to you—in that sense. But you must help me to arrange, to plan to—do the other. I've no one else to turn to; I haven't had any one since——" She blushed. "You must help me against yourself."

"All right!" returned Rignold with dreary readiness, from some outer place. He had been wishing himself far away somewhere in space, like

155

Aleck. He would exist for her if he could die, perhaps. But he added, " We'll keep up the fight !"

She contemplated him for a moment reflectively. " No," she said. " I will. But you mustn't. The town is right, perhaps, but whether it's right or wrong, we couldn't go on together if they think—that ! No ; I will go on alone, and we will see what happens. I won't believe that every one has deserted me all at once. I won't believe that towns, as you say, have no gratitude, and no memories. Why, memory is the life of a town : how can it look forward to a good future if it forgets its good past ? I'll fight it, and I'll fight it on that line, Ben. I'll *make* them remember ! They shall learn that if they're going to forget Alexander Chester, they've got to do it publicly and shamefully and to my face."

" You *have* got sand !"

" I've got the sand to be true, and if I've got to be true that way—why, I must ; that's all. There's no one else."

" Why, Berna !" he exclaimed in pain.

156

"Oh, Ben! Forgive me. There *is* you, and I know how gladly you'd do it. But don't you see how you're cut off from trying, and how every one is cut off but me? Besides, I'm the one who can do it; it's for him, and that gives me the wisdom and the strength; and it's for him, and I know how he would want it done. But Ben . . . ." Her face lighted up.

"Yes?"

"Listen! This is what you can do for me. I've got an idea. Who has been selected to edit the other paper?"

"Why——"

"I see. They *have* asked you. That makes it so much the simpler!" She leaned forward and touched his arm again. "Edit it, Ben! Edit it!"

"Look here, Berna, what do you take me for? You won't let me be all the friend I'd like to be to you; but I'm not going to make myself your enemy."

"You're going to be twice my friend. Don't

157

you see ? If I must have an opponent, I like you best."

"But I should have to fight you, Berna."

"Of course. But you'd fight fair. The other man might not."

He regarded her for a moment, stupefied, while many thoughts raced through his head. "All right !" he said at last. "All right ! You're giving me a hard row to hoe, and yourself a still harder. Goodness knows how you'll get out the paper from a rocking-chair, with nobody to help you. But I suppose you'll manage somehow. You've got the pluck for *anything*."

"Good ! Then that's settled. Now tell me, who is fomenting this trouble ? "

Berna would still have liked a good, round, sham-literary word on her way to the stake, and Rignold's directness would still have been puzzled and amused by it. He half smiled now as he told her that McDermott, of the Chicago Clothing House, B. G. Franks, the shoe man Martin, of the European Hotel, Beck Kruger,

158

the grocer (who she would remember was
always taking a column in the *Telepheme* to
announce the arrival of a fresh consignment of
Grand Junction peaches), and Dibble, the lately
appointed postmaster, were at the head of the
movement for a new paper.

"What!" she exclaimed, "Mr. Dibble one
of the recreants—the man who took my father's
place, the man for whose appointment we
worked so hard on the *Telepheme*, Ben? You're
mistaken!" He shook his head. "But they
have all pretended they were my friends.
Don't you remember how enthusiastic Martin
was at first? And McDermott? They took
half a column apiece, though neither of them
needed it, and promised to stand by the paper
through thick and thin. They thought I could
be useful to them then, I suppose; and now
they think some one else will be. That's all.
No matter, Ben." She gave him her hand.
" *You* be the some one else! I'll promise not
to hate you. But I'll fight you tooth and nail,

until—*until I know.* The day I can make myself sure, the day I feel I can face Aleck without shame, and say : ' The town doesn't want us,' and know I say truth—that day I give the paper up. The day I know that the *Telepheme* can't help the town, I shall know it will hinder it, and I will never publish another issue. Till then it's war ! "

She smiled a pallid smile from among her pillows, as she shook hands again, and he saw that she had overstrained herself.

" Good-night."

" Good-night, Berna. Good-night ! We sha'n't meet any more for talks about the paper. I suppose we sha'n't meet at all except in editorials, where we'll give each other down the banks. I'm sorry. The worst, though, is being afraid for you. For God's sake, take care of yourself ! "

Berna looked up at him shrewdly. " You think I'll be careless about my health, and over-tax my strength, with no monitor by to keep me straight. Well, then, I promise you I'll be careful. That shall be my thanks for all the care you've taken of me, Ben. *I* can't afford to be ungrateful ! " she added wistfully ; " I haven't friends enough. Good-night,—dear, kind Ben ! "

III.

HE got himself out ; and the next morning went to the committee whose advances he had declined and told them that, if they were still of the same mind, he would undertake the editorship of the paper and furnish the capital. That afternoon he telegraphed East for a balance of his savings, amounting to $600—all that he had remaining in the world ; and when the money arrived he bought the necessary materials—type press, paper, and office furniture—opened his office in the Bloxham Block, opposite the office of the *Telepheme*, and published the first issue of the *Apex*. The name, which was chosen as a tribute to the fact that Rustler lay under the shadow of the Continental Divide, was suggested by Dibble, the postmaster, who saw a kind of dual symbolism in it.

"'Apex' means on top, don't it?" said Dibble. "Well, then! And ain't Rustler on top—on top of the backbone of the Continent, on top of her rivals, on top when it comes to railroads, on the tip-top when it comes to newspapers? That's right—'Apex' it is."

Rignold didn't care what they called it; it was his paper, but it was *her* experiment. His care was for the paper itself; and he took immense pains with the first issue.

"Oh, well!" explained Dibble, "who ever heard of a first issue being much? The machinery don't work, the type's all fresh, the staff hasn't settled to work, the whole thing's loose. That's been true of every paper from the beginning of the world. It'll shake down! It'll shake down! Trust Rignold for that. He's the stuff. Why, it's worth two of that measly female sheet across the road, now. We'll get a railroad with this paper, and we'll get some sense about politics. No woman business ! "

But the first number of the *Apex* was really not so much better than the *Telepheme* which Berna published the same day ; being set in larger type, it contained less news ; the miscellany was made up from " plate matter," as Rignold had always urged that the *Telepheme's* should be ; and there was no such extravagance as Berna's telegraphic letter from Denver. There was more advertising in the *Apex* than in the *Telepheme*, because the business men, having decided on a new paper, threw all their advertising into Rignold's hands ; and though Berna ordered all the " dead " patent medicine cuts in the office, and all the old land office notices that remained standing, to be inserted as fresh advertising, her advertisement columns still looked rather hollow. But this gave her so much the more room for news (which she had now learned to make of the Rustler standard) and for miscellany, in the matter of which her judicious habit of selection went far. On the whole, as the town would have said, if it had not been trying hard to say the other thing, the *Telepheme* was "the better nickel's worth."

Her editorial was an embodiment of what she had said to Rignold, expressed with dignity and with just sufficient feeling. It was extremely direct and uncompromising, though tactful, and if the organisers of the new paper did not wince that evening upon their hearthstones, it was because they had determined not to in advance. That which really troubled them was the perception, forced upon them with the second issue of the *Apex*, that the *Telepheme* was not yet stamped out, nor very obviously in a way to be. They had taken Berna's editorial for her swan-song, believing that, in depriving her of the assistance of Rignold, they had adopted the surest mode of stopping a paper which had become an injury to the good standing of the town. But Berna went on, with depleted advertising columns, but with ever-fattening news columns, and with a resolved and untroubled air which invited victory, if it did not predict it. At Rignold's suggestion, she had found a substitute for Barton, who, released from his mechanical duties, gathered local news for her, and looked after the advertising. Barton could not actually replace Rignold, but, in common with many Western men, he balanced an incapacity to do anything very well by an inability to do anything very badly ; and soon discovered that faculty for thinning out one local item into four, and imagining one out of nothing, which is the bulwark of the Rural Press. With his help Berna got out a very creditable paper. Removed from the office, and informed only by Barton's report of the system by which the matter outside her own department was gathered, she was often driven to wonder, as she held a fresh issue in her hand, where all the good things had come from. Her judgment told her that it was in fact quite as presentable a sheet as in the good days when Rignold was by her side; but though she would have been glad to believe this for the sake of the future, she denied it to herself resolutely, with a sentiment of loyalty to her old associate; and out of the same feeling, coupled with a knightly unwillingness to think ill of a rival, put away from her the doubt whether the *Apex* was, after all, as good a paper as her own.

Rignold had never worked harder than he was now working on the *Apex*. He had never reached the *Telepheme* office so early as he now reached the office of the *Apex*, nor left it so late. He had promised himself not to see Berna again for a long time to come; his news of her came by wa of the town. All that he knew of her was gathered from observation of the outside of her home, as he passed it, morning and night, on his way to or from his canvas-roofed cabin on Ticknor's Mountain. Three months passed without giving him a sight of her, until, passing her house after midnight one night on his way home from the office, he saw a light burning in her bedroom, on the upper floor, and knew that she was sitting up, writing. The gravel which he threw softly against the pane brought her instantly to the window. For a moment she looked bewilderingly about in the un-accustomed darkness, straining her eyes first upon the road where Rignold was standing in the shadow, and then over toward the huge black frame of Ticknor's, swelling up behind the opposite row of houses, and darkening against the starless sky.

" Well, *Telepheme ?* "

The figure in the window drew back startled ; but in a moment the answer came softly :

" Well, *Apex ?* "

He came out of the shadow.

" Is that you, Ben ? "

" Yes ! " said Rignold. " Remember your promise."

" What ? "

" Go to bed ! "

"Oh!" She laughed; and her laugh seemed to Rignold to widen musically into the night in waves of pure joy. "All right!' She leaned out of the window for a moment in silence. "Why aren't you in bed yourself?"

"Been fighting you."

"Well, that takes time. How's the *Apex?*"

"Blooming. How's yours?"

"I've lost a good deal of advertising."

"They tell me half the circulation's gone. Is that true?"

"Yes. But my courage isn't—nor my money. I think I like aggression."

"Hope the *Apex* gives you plenty."

"Yes; enough. But I don't want to beg off. Ben!"

"Well?"

"I'm glad we made that arrangement. You give me all I want to do sometimes; but you *do* fight fair!"

"I've got a scorcher on you in my next '

"Have you?"

"Yes!"

"Then I must go to work. Good-night, Ben!"

"Oh, see here, Berna ; don't do that!"

"Do you want me to let the *Apex* have it all it's own way?"

"No; but you ain't going to do any more work to-night. Look here—I'll put it off to the issue after next."

"Well! Will it keep?"

"Keep? An article against you? Like ice at zero?"

"Then I won't prepare my answer till next week. Good-night.—Oh, Ben!"

"Well?"

"I'm preparing a surprise for the *Apex*."

"No?"

"Yes. You remember my speaking of that girl with the strange character, who used to go to school with me at Kansas City before I went East to Miss Drewett's—Dodo McFarlane?

She's just married to Mr. Mutrie, the president
of the Three C's, and she's coming here on her
wedding journey. I had her letter to-day, and
I've written to invite them to stay here with
me."

Rignold allowed an expressive whistle to
escape into the darkness.

" It *is* interesting, isn't it?" continued Berna.

"Interesting? It's a scare-head sensation
news item. I'll have to get to work myself.
Good-night !"

She leaned a little further out of the window.
" You won't divulge my secret, of course. I'm
keeping it to surprise the town."

" Oh, I won't give you away. Go to bed !"

" I will. I'm so glad to have seen you again,
Ben."

" That's right. Good-night !"

He disappeared up the dark road, and Berna
closed her window.

When Rignold reached the Bloxham Block
next morning he found Dibble in the narrow

stall he had partitioned off from the composing-room for his office. His visitor dropped his feet from the table to the floor as he entered, and rose, folding up a copy (Berna and Rignold of course exchanged) of the last issue of the *Tele-pheme*. Dibble shook himself down into his trousers with a frown.

" Morning," said he.

Rignold nodded as he swept a space clear on his desk, and settled down to work.

" Been losing Hymee, the hatter," I see," continued his visitor, dusting his hand with Berna's paper.

" Mr. Hymee has seen fit to withdraw his advertisement, if that's what you mean, Mr Dibble."

" Yes; I've been around to see him this morning. He says he wants to see our paper succeed. He ain't got nothing against it, and he ain't going to support our lady contemporary anyway. But, 'See here, now,' he says, 'your paper——"

"*My* paper, please, Mr. Dibble."

"Well, yours, if you like to call it so."

"I like to stick to facts, if it's all the same to you. Has anybody got a dime in the *Apex* besides me?"

"Certainly not. But we feel as if we were supporting you. I suppose you don't mind our holding up your hands?"

"Not if you leave them free," returned Rignold, whirling about in his swivel seat, tilting it back, and thrusting his hands into his pockets. "What does Hymee say?"

Dibble did the *Telepheme* up into a newspaper-carrier's wad, as if he were meditating throwing it over a subscriber's fence into a front yard, before he answered: "Why, it's this way. Hymee says that woman-mush across the way, that some folks in this town call a newspaper, is knocking the stuffing out of us fellows, and we don't know what's happening to us. He's opposed on principle to a lady paper, but he goes in for straight talk, and he says there ain't no comparison between the *Apex* and the *Telepheme*, and that every one says so."

"That's just what we've always supposed, ain't it?"

"Not Hymee's way. He tried to prove to me that there wasn't the hustle of a dead steer about our whole outfit ; he says the *Apex*, as at present conducted, hasn't fire enough to keep a corner warm in hell, nor the romp and the razzle-dazzle to run an engine down a two-hundred-foot grade, let alone pulling the Three C's into Rustler. Now, don't get riled ! He didn't mean you, of course."

"I'm all right, Mr. Dibble," said Rignold, raising his eyebrows. "Go on."

"That's all. But it occurred to me—— I was wondering——"

"Yes. Well?"

"He's away off. *We* know that. But it simply occurred to me that it was a sort of hint. Perhaps we *could* put more——"

"Work?"

"No, sir. You *work*. But more roar and slam-bang, more git up and howl. That's what does the business !"

Rignold surveyed him thoughtfully for a moment, as a silence fell.

"Do you want to buy the paper, Mr. Dibble ?"

"Well, no—no. I can't say as I do."

"Know any one else that wants to buy it ?"

"No."

"All right, then. I'll run it myself. Good morning."

Two more small advertisements were withdrawn within a week from the *Apex;* and the day after the publication of the succeeding issue, B. G. Franks, dealer in boots and shoes, who had been one of Rignold's original supporters, called at the office to say that he felt forced to withdraw his advertisement temporarily, as an expression of his disapproval of the course of the *Apex;* but should be happy to restore it as soon as Rignold saw his way to making a better paper. Rignold perceived

Dibble's hand in this, and smiled ; it was what Dibble would have called "bringing pressure." No more advertisements from members of the original committee were discontinued ; but subscriptions began to fall off. Even from the surrounding country orders reached Rignold to stop the paper ; and no new subscriptions were recorded.

A month later, when Mutrie reached Topaz with his young bride, and stopped over a day, Rustler gnashed its teeth. Dibble, who had now turned frankly against Rignold, swore outright. The news was discussed on the corners of the mountain street by excited groups, like another Bull Run. It represented, stated in the soberest terms, nothing less than disaster to the town that the President of the Three C's should stop at Topaz, and not so much as pass through Rustler. A committee, consisting of Dibble, McDermott, and Franks, was formed to go down to Topaz by the afternoon train, and invite the President to at least take a look

at the town. But before they could start,
Berna, who had been holding back her edition
of that week for a telegram from Mrs. Mutrie,
making all sure, got the *Telepheme* upon the
streets. It set forth her news so modestly that
at first no one would believe it. The office of
the paper was instantly filled with inquirers—
Dibble among the first.

"She's got a telegram, I tell you!" said
Barton.

"Shoot your telegram! Let's see it!"

Barton left them clamouring, and went to ask
Berna's permission. As he came back up the
street, holding the fluttering bit of paper aloft
in his hand, the group outside of the office gave
an uncertain cheer; then, as Dibble snatched it
and read it aloud, they howled with glee. Some
were for going straight to Berna's house, and
offering her the cheers at closer quarters;
but every one was in favour of a drink, and for
the moment it resolved itself into that. It was
about eleven o'clock that night when a little

176

torch-light procession made its way to Berna's house, and relieved in complimentary song its enthusiasm, its happiness, its renewed goodwill to Berna, and perhaps a little shame-faced repentance and regret.

She was obliged at last to appear in her doorway; but, apparently overcome by emotion, could say nothing until, as she stood swaying on the threshold, she caught sight of Rignold's white face in the midst of the flickering lights on the fringe of the crowd. Then, plucking up courage, she began tremblingly :

" FELLOW-TOWNSMEN,—I am grateful to you for this unexpected honour. Believe me, it touches me deeply. But I must not, even for a moment, take it to myself. It belongs, you and I both know, wholly to another. I lay it proudly at the feet of Alexander Chester."

Rignold's face suddenly disappeared, and a voice from the crowd shouted. " No ! no !" As she lost sight of the sustaining eye on the outmost circle of her audience, something seemed to give way within her ; the denial roused her, however.

"But I say 'Yes.' Let no one, thinking to please me, refuse to Alexander Chester the praise and the reward that are so utterly his due, and which belong to him, and him alone. Fellow-townsmen, it was he who first fought your battle for the railroad ; it was he who first led you to dream of the possibility of bringing the Three C's to Rustler ; it was he whose ringing words, going forth from week to week in the columns of his paper, have made the coming of the road practical, and realisable, and near ; and he it was, too, whose labours for the town, in co-operation with the strong and willing hands of those I see before me to-night, have brought Rustler to a position where she *deserves* the railroad." ("Good ! Deserves ! That's the ticket !" murmured the crowd.) "Whatever I may have been able to do has merely been in humble following of his footsteps. If he had not lived, in all human probability, none of us would be here to-night. When you say a word in praise of me, I must take it, therefore, as intended to be two for him ; for he is not only the source and inspiration of everything that I may do, but even in death he watches over us—the guide, the counsellor, the Captain of our town !"

She paused ; and the crowd burst into wild cheers.

"The Captain ! Hip ! Hip ! Hurrah ! Hurrah ! Hurrah ! *Tiger !*"

Berna smiled upon them from her doorway— beatified.

IV.

An hour later, against all protests from her mother, she left her home for the first time in many months. Strength came to her with her need ; that one sweet little moment of success, which compensated for all that she had borne for the town, and for all she had suffered at its hands, seemed to give a lost physical soundness

179

and courage back to her. She felt strong enough for anything ; and, with that wine of happiness coursing through her veins, she certainly felt strong enough to drive to Barton's. The depression of the past months, since the launching of the *Apex*, had made her nervous and doubtful about prosperity ; she dared not trust any one to take it by the hand but herself. To be ready for the demand on the morrow, she meant to get Barton to go to the office and to print at once, before morning, on Aleck's old hand-press, five hundred copies of the new issue of the *Telepheme;* and to make quite sure, she meant to drive to the office with him, and see the fresh edition started. The paper had not been obliged to print twice since Aleck's time. She must watch her boom. Her heart beat high.

At Barton's there was no one but his wife. She said her husband was already at the office.

"Seems to me," she lamented, "he's always at that office ! I suppose his new work's a good thing ; but it takes him away a sight of

time. I don't believe he's been a night at home
since he began it ! "

Berna wondered, but drove on, drawing her
wraps tight around her against the unaccus-
tomed air. Except for the lights at the European Hotel and at the Elegant Booze, the
Honeycomb, and Uncle Dick's, the town was
dark. Straggling groups from the serenading
party still paraded the streets, singing, and
lurching noisily in each other's arms. Berna
gazed meditatively at the dusky roofs of the
town to which she had given a year's loving service, and which she had not seen since the
warm, sunny morning when she had driven with
Aleck to the station to take the train. The
town knew her now ; but what difference if it
did not ? *He* knew !

As she toiled up the dark staircase leading to
the *Telepheme* office, supporting herself by her
stick, a crack of light shone into her eyes from
under the door ; and she heard the old press
jammed down sharply within. Barton had

plainly guessed her thought and gone silently to work. How good every one was to her !

She turned the knob and went in. A gush of light greeted her. The place was all illumined. Barton was at the press ; the boy was hurrying about. From the inner room a voice she knew cried out :

"We shall have to put that silver editorial over to the issue after next, Barton. Our next issue will have to be a kind of Jubilee Mutrie number—editorials, locals, everything. I'll do the squibs this week and an account of the President's visit, if you'll look after my regular locals."

"All right !" responded Barton from his press. After a moment he looked up and saw Berna standing there.

"Why, Miss Dexter !" he exclaimed, mechanically stopping the press. He came toward her, wiping his hand, which, however, he finally wrapped in a corner of his printer's apron and offered to her that way.

"You ought to have sent for me," he said, abstractedly.

She looked at him for a moment.

"Who's in there?"

"What?" asked Barton, offering her a chair, with a doubtful glance over his shoulder.

She pointed.

"Oh, there! Nobody, I guess."

"Will you do me a favour, Mr. Barton?"

"Yes, of course. I don't know."

"Take this chair." Barton seated himself, and stared after her as she pushed quickly into the room where Rignold sat writing busily at his old desk, which was littered with proofs and manuscript.

"Berna!" he exclaimed, looking up as she entered.

"Ben Rignold, what are you doing here?"

"Getting up a little copy. I often come on here of an evening to do my work, from old habit. You don't mind, I hope?"

"You mean *my* work?"

183

"I didn't say so."

"You don't need to. I heard you just now give your order to Barton. Ben! Ben!— You're just wicked!"

Tears filled her eyes. She sat down suddenly.

"Let me move those," he said, rising, and coming to her quickly; and she saw that she had seated herself on a chair heaped with a pile of old exchanges. He moved them to another chair, avoiding her eyes, which followed him everywhere. As he took his seat again under the lamp, which threw down a strong writing light upon the table, she saw how worn he looked. There were purple rings under his eyes, and his face was drawn. His disordered hair, which he had probably tumbled as he wrote, gave him a wild look. It was three months since she had seen him closely, by daylight. She reproached herself bitterly.

"You're too good to breathe!" she murmured, in continuance of her indictment, as she fastened her eyes on him. "How dared you? Why didn't you tell me?"

"See here, Berna! Why didn't you stay at home? Then you wouldn't have known."

"Well, I'm glad enough I came," she said, still breathless.

"Well, then, I ain't."

"So it's you, Ben Rignold, who have been making my paper better than the *Apex !*" she went on, unheeding. "It's been you from the beginning." She stopped suddenly, startled. "Then it must be you, too, who have made the *Apex* so bad!" she added.

Rignold smiled. "Did you think it was bad?"

"Never till now. I never let myself. But I know now that it's been the worst paper in the State!"

"Did you expect me to make it the best, with your paper across the way?"

"I didn't expect you to make *mine* the best! Oh, Ben!"

"Pshaw! That was easy!" he said, laughing. "The trouble's been to make the *Apex* poor enough without giving the scheme away. I've always been afraid that you'd tumble, if the town didn't. Come, Berna! You didn't suppose I was working at that rate to *succeed*, did you?"

"I thought——" began Berna, tremulously.

"Then take it back, please! The man who couldn't succeed, with that paper and that backing, by smoking cigars in his rear office, ought to give up the business. To make such a paper *fail* takes work!"

"Ben!" she exclaimed. "You've ruined yourself!"

"Oh no, I haven't. But I've ruined the *Apex*. The Sheriff is to pay me a visit to-morrow. Nobody knows it yet; but I may as well tell you, because it'll be all out in the morning. I *had* hoped to fail last week. But I couldn't

186

get enough advertisements and subscriptions dropped."

She looked thoughtfully at him for a full moment. "Ben, I believe you're the best man in the world," she said, solemnly.

"I guess not," laughed Rignold, uneasily.

"You are," she repeated. "And, Ben——"

"Yes?"

"You mustn't fail!"

"But I've got it all fixed. After to-morrow there won't be but one paper in Rustler."

"That's what I mean," she said, huskily· "Let's *make* it one! Let's . . . . consolidate!"

"Berna!"

"Well?" she answered, looking down with a deep blush.

He came and stood over her, and laid a hand upon her chair. "Berna, do you mean it?"

She looked up with tears streaming down her face.

"I guess so."

"And Aleck?"

She smiled happily through her tears as she laid a hand in his.

" Ben, dear, *we* will keep up the fight ! "

Printed by BALLANTYNE HANSON & CO.
London and Edinburgh

W. B.
1861-1891.

No higher tribute to the memory of my dear friend and colleague, Wolcott Balestier, could have been paid than by the allusions to his extraordinary mind and character which have been made by the eminent writers who were in constant contact with him. It will, I hope, not be thought out of place for me to add a word in affectionate remembrance of the delightful and invigorating intercourse with him which I was privileged to enjoy during the last years of his life. Joined with him in work which brought us together daily, I had a rare opportunity of knowing the man—of admiring his nature, full as it was of disinterested kindness, and of wondering at the surprising courage with which he sought difficulties for the satisfaction of successfully overcoming them. He ignored the possibility of failure in anything to which he gave his mind. No one more than myself could feel the blank left by his death, and it seems too much to hope that even in time this blank can be filled.

                    WILLIAM HEINEMANN.